LULU

LULU

by

NANCY FRIDAY

Copyright © 2012 Nancy Friday
Publisher: Nancy Friday

All rights reserved. No part of this book shall be reproduced or transmitted in any form or by any means, electronic or mechanical, including photocopying, recording, or by any information storage and retrieval system, without prior written permission of the publisher, except where permitted by law. For more information contact: Robert Thixton, Pinder Lane & Garon-Brooke Associates, Ltd. 159 West 53rd Street, New York, N.Y. 10019
e-mail: pinderl@rcn.com

Print ISBN: 978-0-786-75446-5
eISBN: 978-0-786-75447-2

This is a work of fiction. Names, characters and incidents either are the product of the author's imagination or are used fictitiously. Any resemblance to actual events, persons, living or dead, is entirely coincidential.

Cover art: Roger Hayes

CHAPTER ONE
1 9 4 6

The house was pink, the shutters blue and the lovely thing looked to grow right out of the sidewalk along with all the other houses, each a different pastel than the one before, marching like a rainbow into the near distance. "Follow," it said, and follow she did, pointing her Mary Janes towards the rainbow's end, which is how Lulu began her new life in the fairy tale place to which they had driven for three days from the dark, sad city up north.

Only nine-year-old Harry saw Lulu leave the car they were unpacking, carrying suitcases and packages into the pink house, lovely enough through the open door but not as magnetic as the rainbow of houses.

"Where are you going, Lulu? Come back!" he called, then gave it up, no more anxious than she in this fairy tale place.

In the fullest comfort ever known in her four years, she felt the place put an arm around her. "Walk the rainbow," it said and she had got out of the car, assured that nothing bad could happen if she walked past the blue house, turned the corner at the yellow or entered the dusty grocery store where a gentle dark-skinned man behind the counter took her nickel for a Milky Way.

"You all right, chile?" he asked, smiling and looking down at the little girl, all legs and arms, her dark hair pulled tightly into braids, the gold rimmed glasses slipping off her nose, and the sash of her wrinkled dress untied so that its ends dragged behind her.

"Oh, yes," Lulu replied, staring at his gold tooth and his skin the color of her mother's pocketbook. She told him they had been driving for three days and, because he was so interested in her story, Lulu decided to eat her Milky Way in the store. She said they had seen little children his color when they stopped for gas and that the man at the pump had told her, "That's Gullah they talkin.' Toss 'em some pennies and they go away." Which is what Lulu had done, prompting the children to offer a song and dance, giving her such a nice feeling indeed.

At this point in her story, Lulu patted the pocket of her dress where she kept the tiny change purse embroidered with flowers, a pretty thing she had admired on her grandmother's dressing table. "You keep it," Grandy had said, putting a few coins in it just before they had left the Dark City up north. "You're never too young to learn respect for money." Four years of watching her mother handle money with deep sighs that said, "Oh, I really don't like touching this," had taught Lulu that money must be "powerful medicine," as Tonto said to The Lone Ranger. Very well, Lulu had concluded, if Grandy is "made of money"—a phrase Lulu had overheard, leaving her with dream sleep images of her grandmother stuffed like a bank with coins—then I shall be like her. Which is how Lulu came to be a saver of pennies. Life was teaching her that it was better to be like her grandmother who was "made of money," than her mother who sighed when she handled it.

The candy bar eaten, Lulu stopped outside the screen door and once again the pretty picture of the place into which they had fallen, like Dorothy in "The Wizard of Oz," filled her with pleasure. Then she recited the route she had walked away from the pink house. Take a right and then another right, memory said, which she did with the seasoned traveler's assurance. Thus did she stake her claim, marking Charleston her own, an instinctual homing device that would return her to the pink house for the rest of her life. Sure enough, there was her brother Harry, standing on the sidewalk, watching her now with his sweet smile, though he shook his head as if to say, "What am I going to do with you?"

Beside Harry stood a large woman, the same color as the man in the store, though she was much bigger around and her hair was tied up in a bright scarf that matched her dress over which was a white apron wide as a tablecloth. The big woman looked from Lulu to Harry. "That's Lulu," he said and the woman's anxious face creased into smiles. She opened her arms and Lulu happily walked into them. "Where you been, chile? You no sooner in a strange place, you go walkin' here, there, everywhere?" The woman scooped her up and pressed her head against her soft bosom the size of two bolster pillows. "How you find your way to buy candy bars 'n this a new city?" On she scolded, all the love in the world in her voice as she carried her "baby girl" into the pink house, straightening Lulu's pigtails with one hand.

On their way to the kitchen, Lulu could hear her mother's exhausted voice upstairs, arguing with Harry, who didn't want to have his bedroom on the same floor as his mother's, but was insisting his room be on the third floor, down the hall from Lulu's. As much as she wanted to see the rest of this mysterious house with its high ceilings and long shadows reaching through the slats in the shutters closed against the afternoon sun, Lulu decided to stay with her safe harbor whose name was Evangeline. "But you call me Vangie, honey."

In the kitchen, Vangie was taking food out of the refrigerator, down from the cupboard shelves, and talking to Lulu all the while. "I been sent a list a food you like but I got somethin' special Vangie brung for you." She handed Lulu a little box. "Peach leather. Go on, eat some." Lulu put the lovely sticky orange-colored strips into her mouth and said appreciatively, "Yum, yum!" making Vangie laugh.

"Will you sleep here, too?" Lulu asked climbing onto a chair and from there to the counter where she sat watching Vangie peel shrimp and prepare rice.

"Most time I sleep here. My room next to you. Maybe sometime I sleep home. Now, honey girl…" She picked up Lulu in her enormous arms. "Now it time to nap." Vangie carried Lulu up two flights of stairs. Harry had already claimed the room at the top, leaving the two far rooms for Lulu and Vangie, who put Lulu on the bed, took off her shoes, and laid a light blanket over her. "I leave the door to my room open, honey, and I be right here when you wake up."

Thus did gratitude to a place and its people begin reparations, relaxing little shoulders. Can a town lost in time do so much good, so quickly? For the first time in four years, Lulu was convinced that everything would be all right. "You are home now," the place promised, and she took it at its word.

From down the hall that night came the sound of Harry's radio, a wailing horn playing the blues in the night, a lullaby heard from the beginning of her time.

CHAPTER TWO

His name was never spoken. Nor were there photographs of him in whom Lulu might see herself. She was so good that she never asked, "Where is he?"

Nor did she dream of him either by day or night. Every little girl had a father, but it was as if the scouring maid on the bathtub cleanser can had gotten into Lulu's head, deep into the canals of memory, and erased every trace of him.

Her dreams at night were not sweet; yet scary as the bad dreams were, Lulu was addicted to the black and white thrillers at the movies, the blood and guts, monsters, killers, vampires, so long as Harry was beside her in the dark. But the day she and Harry saw "Salome," with John The Baptist's bloody head on the platter, it brought such terror and tears Harry had to buy her two chocolate nut sundaes afterwards. That night her screams woke Vangie who came from her room and held Lulu in her arms. "There, there baby girl, shhh…" Vangie crooned.

"Oh, the bloody head…all that blood and his eyes looking at me… oh, Vangie!"

"It just a movie, baby…."

"No, no, Vangie, I saw his bloody face…. It followed us to Charleston!"

Born into The Great War begun in 1942, Lulu had spent her first four years hearing about missing men, absent fathers gone across the world to fight. It seemed that everyone else was waiting and hoping for daddy, except in other homes there were photos of the man for whom they prayed and an expectation of his homecoming. Songs on the radio, like "I'll Walk Alone," were all about a man gone away; Lulu knew by heart "I'll Be Seeing You," and when she and Harry saw "The White Cliffs of Dover," everyone in the audience cried when a daddy died; and, when the ushers passed a box down the aisles into which people put money for the Red Cross, Harry gave Lulu coins to contribute.

Being part of a community of people that waited for fathers to return, Lulu didn't doubt her father would materialize, maybe without an arm or a leg, but daddy, father, would stand at their door with a duffel bag, needing a hug and a long nap before dinner with everyone at the table, a real family.

Optimism was what songs and movies were about, and Lulu drank it like the stuff of life. She listened to her mother's record, "There'll Be Bluebirds Over The White Cliffs of Dover" over and over. When people smiled at a little girl on her bicycle singing "I'll Get By" in perfect pitch and every word in place, Lulu smiled back and waved, knowing deep in her heart that everyone was waiting for daddies to come home. Believing it was part of what made it come true. Didn't the boy always find his dog in the movies? Didn't Dorothy get back home in "The Wizard of Oz?" Yes, sometimes the man didn't return from war, and they gave the mother or child a folded flag instead of him, but you had to keep believing be-cause sometimes "they" were wrong and you were right to never give up hope. That's what the movies and the songs promised.

When the war did end and the men began to arrive back, Lulu looked to her mother for a sign that her sighing days were over and that Lulu could now breathe more easily. She hoped that soon Penelope would put her arms around her little girl and say something like they said in the movies: "Darling, isn't it wonderful? Your daddy's coming home!" Happy as Lulu would be to have a father, she would be equally grateful to no lon-ger feel herself the source of Penelope's well of sighs. She would no longer think herself a bad girl for hating Harry, the brother whom she also loved; her hatred was a scary feeling that no amount of good deeds put to rest.

He did come home. That much she remembered. But it wasn't like

"The Best Years of Our Lives," when even the soldier who'd lost his hands in battle had a happy ending. No, in Lulu's bank of memories the few happy pictures of her daddy home from the war were squeezed between images so scary as to defy focusing on them. It was safer to leave the past just that.

So that she would not bother her mother, her smile got broader, her list of good deeds longer, and the commandment to never ask about him incised itself even deeper into her soul. Instead of sadness and grief and rage too an infantile crying storm that he wasn't there to love her (as she was absolutely sure he would)—instead of all this, Lulu was good. When her grandmother, Grandy, had decided to send them all down south to this fairytale town, Lulu believed it was her reward for being good.

"You have sweet dreams, baby?" Vangie asked one morning, pouring milk on Lulu's Wheaties.

"Oh, yes," Lulu replied, dutifully forgetting the nightmares. Even in the warm bath of waking up in Charleston, in her dream sleep last night, she had been alone, a spectator.

Later that day a stranger came for tea along with one of Penelope's friends. "And where's your daddy?" the stranger asked Lulu, who answered, "My Daddy's dead." For a moment Lulu thought her mother might add something. But there was a silence until Penelope continued her conversation.

She yearned to ask Harry about their father, yet she could tell that Harry begged for privacy. Just to be sure her mother wouldn't also disappear, Lulu began to watch her like a hawk and eavesdrop on her conversations. So successfully did Lulu feign her disinterest that years later her mother would say, "You never asked about your father. I assumed you didn't want to know."

* * *

So simple and un-trafficked was the grid of Charleston's streets and so kind were its people that Lulu was allowed to roam alone. This particular day, she decided to walk a square, meaning to keep turning right until she got back home, which is how she came upon the church just around the corner from the pink house. She had seen the tall spire from her bedroom window but never knew it was so close. Because the church's carved doors stood open and the singing voices of the choir beckoned, Lulu walked in.

It was a weekday and the choir was rehearsing for Easter Sunday; no one saw the small figure walk down the aisle, turn into a pew and sit. Lulu watched the reverence given to the man on the cross. Poor man, she thought, dying all alone, and no daddy on earth, just one to pray to in Heaven, like me.

The minister found her sitting in rapt attention after the singing was over, and introduced her to the choirmaster, the organist, and the choir members. As was customary in Charleston, everyone had time to spend with a child. Quizzed by the choirmaster as to where she lived, Lulu pointed beyond the graveyard that dated back to before The War For Southern Independence and said, "I live on the other side of the wall." Then the choirmaster walked her home, much to the relief of Vangie who stood waiting anxiously outside the pink house.

"I'm going to Sunday school and then to Church," Lulu announced. That day, she decided that Grandy must have sent them to Charleston for one reason: so that she, Lulu, could invent a new life with a happy beginning and herself as the happiest little girl in Charleston. From this day on Lulu went to church every Sunday, where she prayed for her father. Church felt so good she began to sing and pray for the man on the cross too, joining her voice with His cries to His father. The opening chords of "Eternal Father Strong To Save," always made her cry.

CHAPTER THREE

1948

Charleston was made for a child on a secret mission, the whole town in an extended state of elegant repose since the great war of the 1860s. Modern commerce and industry had passed it by, though freighters still docked down at the waterfront, a short walk from Lulu's front door. The large paving blocks on the sidewalks sloped gracefully towards the narrow streets barely alive with traffic. Every other house had the slightest tilt and at least one in each block had its windows boarded over, promising revelation for a six-year-old raised on half-finished sentences, whispers, and questions no one dared answer.

With so much mystery came an invitation to explore, and Lulu didn't hesitate to peek through the boarded-over window of the house down the street; all she could see were blue walls faded pale except where pictures once had hung. It looked so lonely, she could have sworn she heard: "Enter." The boards on one window were loose and were about to fall off anyway, so she helped them along and climbed into the dusty blue room. Down the hall was a kitchen with unwashed dishes in the sink, and, in the next room, what looked like a pile of rags turned out to be an old woman surrounded by her cats. A shaft of sunlight misted with dust made it hard to distinguish the elderly, dark-skinned woman's bandannaed head amidst the rags and cats.

"Hey," said Lulu, squatting, holding out her hand to the kittens though her eyes never left the terrified old woman's face. "I'm Lulu. Are your cats hungry?"

"We all hongry," whispered old Flossy, and the terms of the friendship were forged. That day, Lulu ran home, stole some food, ran back to Flossy, and fed her and her cats. Flossy became Lulu's first responsibility, her excuse for breaking her mother's rules. Like the forbidden highest limbs of a tree and the Do Not Enter signs, the food that Lulu smuggled out of Vangie's well-stocked kitchen was a clue she believed was planted for her on purpose.

In the movies at the Palace, the Germans and the Japs were demons. "Our Boys" were young and brave, whether lying dead on a battlefield or walking down the streets of Charleston in their sailor suits. Good people held doors open for you, begged your pardon when they inadvertently stepped in front of you in a line. Good children shot to their feet when elders entered the room.

Goodness and manners defined this city of churches and bright sunlight, or maybe it was simply that there had been too many long shadows to have seen any goodness in The Dark City. One morning Lulu prowled the waterfront where freight cars stood in a vast lot overgrown with weeds. The sign alone, No Trespassing, was irresistible. Any anxiety at entering either the railway cars or the boarded-over warehouses only heightened her determination to not be like her anxious mother. Charleston's rotting wharves with their missing planks and handrails covered in years of seagull dung drove away her sadness and rage. Nothing erased the bad feelings like acts of daring do.

Her few years in the world had taught Lulu that feelings of rage would ruin her chances at getting what she wanted most. Better to go outside and secretly explore forbidden places. Better to make herself as lovable as possible. If she could make herself good enough, no one else would ever leave her. If anyone left, it would be she.

As life brightened, she forgot the bad feelings brought from the Dark City. Only when the voice on the radio warned, "The Shadow knows…," followed by the bloodcurdling laugh, did Lulu freeze in terror. Still, she couldn't resist listening to the program. And when the Sunday school teacher read aloud about the lepers in the Bible hiding themselves in shame, again Lulu felt so guilty that later the same night she had dreamed the nightmare from The Dark City, images that rose from the grave as in the vampire movies which Lulu loved and hated. Awakening from the nightmare, she cried out, and when Vangie rushed into the room said, "I'm sorry, I'm so sorry, please Vangie, won't God forgive me?" and her nurse rocked her until the bad feelings succumbed to sleep saying, "My Lulu ain't done no bad thing, not my baby girl."

Lulu's father was a mystery promising discovery only if she followed the clues carelessly left by her mother. There was, for instance, in her mother's wallet, a tiny photograph of a young man and woman taken in a penny arcade. Was that her mother, so young, and he her father? But the photo had over time glued itself to the leather and to show it to Penelope would expose Lulu as a snoop. And in her mother's lingerie drawer there was a gold ring with two hearts entwined: Penelope and the Phantom? Oh, Lulu would have loved to have that ring!

The search was everything. Lulu was drawn to locked doors, drawers filled with yellowed papers, keys to unknown places. Charleston was an explorer's paradise. Not only was the town old, but it also was small enough for a child to go through microscopically, and it smelled of things hidden away, unseen for generations. Miraculously, its people were pleased to accompany her to their attics or basements where the best secrets live. "Why, that's a good idea," an elderly neighbor said one day when Lulu suggested visiting her attic. "I've been meaning to clean out that dusty old place." Lulu's heart raced at the prospect of unearthing a clue to a mystery.

Left alone in the old woman's living room for a moment, Lulu went to a desk and opened all of its drawers; she took nothing and, had she been discovered in her search, would have truthfully said, "I was just looking."

One evening, Lulu attached herself to a couple out for a stroll and accompanied them home. In another time and place, this would be dangerous, but not then, not there. The three of them made a supper of sandwiches and then they listened to the radio, Fred Allen and the news. She went home with an invitation to return any time, and a promise that next time they would investigate the attic. There was nothing she wanted for herself except the search.

Penelope was not an unkind woman. Wasn't she always there? The sad look on her young face had all but disappeared in the short time they had been in Charleston, though it took only a polite question regarding the whereabouts of her husband to restore anxiety to the grey-green eyes, so becoming with her pale complexion, her auburn hair brushed up into a crown of soft waves.

Lulu saw how much her mother loved the mirror, sought it out upon entering a room. To capture her attention, Lulu sometimes stood behind her mother, coupling their mirrored images. Still Penelope rarely acknowledged her.

Harry and their mother shared a similar beauty, the same grey-green eyes and identical Roman nose. Lulu's nose was so small her glasses were always slipping off and her hair straight as a board and "dark black like an injun," Vangie had proclaimed the first morning she braided Lulu's hair.

"Why doesn't mother see me?" Lulu asked Vangie one day when she was collecting food for Flossie and her cats. Vangie just shook her head.

That Penelope was disinclined to spend time with small children didn't stand out as abnormal in Charleston where black nurses raised their charges day and night. And in the end Lulu couldn't criticize her mother for how life was turning out, given its rich, full course.

One day on her way home from the movie at the Bijou, Lulu came upon a truck that heaved in and out like a beast and made a groaning noise; people had lined up on the sidewalk to pass through the truck and donate money to the Red Cross. Lulu joined the line and saw a woman in a hospital bed looking up at her by way of a mirror. The truck was a huge bellows, keeping her alive by pumping air into her as in a giant sigh. From then on, Lulu knew she had to both guard her mother and save herself, otherwise Penelope would just stop breathing. But then, just as one of her mother's exhalations threatened to go on forever, the cocktail hour would arrive, and Penelope's friends would change her into a pretty woman who laughed. From her vantage on the stairway, Lulu gazed down, needing to believe in this animated image rather than that of a woman who sighed each breath as though it were the last.

While continuing to stand sentinel as Penelope's protector, Lulu felt an irresistible need to get out of her mother's house. Only when Lulu was out of the house did she feel an absolute sureness that she had done nothing to make her mother sigh.

As for the deep responsibility felt for the bad things she'd done in the past, Lulu had no idea what they were. She vowed to make up for them by bringing home nothing but straight A's, along with comments her teachers saying she was special. When good marks, along with her elected offices as president of the class and captain of the team, failed to stop Penelope's sighs, Lulu gave up hope that her mother would change.

One day at her best friend Fanny's, the six-year-old Lulu sat on the toilet seat lid and hungrily watched Fanny's mother wash her daughter's hair, then wrap her head in a big soft towel. As the mother's gentle hands untangled the hair, her daughter's head rested against her breast as it clearly had since their time together began. All the stuffing went out of Lulu, and she froze, anguished.

She tried with all her might to be Lulu the Good though she knew otherwise. Where the bad feelings came from she wasn't sure, but putting on a smiling face was so successful she began to believe she really was that girl. Fear was something else she could not allow herself given that her mother was afraid of everything, so Lulu tried to be fearless like her nurse Vangie. But the nightmares laughed at her childish defenses.

Scary as life in The Dark City up north had been, there was a promise of absolute solidity in Charleston. Here manners were the glue that held society together, and were never lost, not even in the great war between North and South. To be part of this solid world, Lulu became its people, in no way more than their manners. Soon she was eager to give up her seat on the bus to an older person, to tell her friends' parents how delicious the dinner was and wasn't the day lovely and, of course, bolting to her feet when a grown-up entered the room, answering every adult with a "Yes, ma'am" or a "No, sir." The very doing of it, saying it, brought a joy. The healing process was called manners.

Soon brightness bleached the bad memories until they faded into for-getfulness, leaving only a few dark images that Penelope would later swear hadn't happened. "No, Lulu, there was never an argument around the breakfast table, never broken glass and you underneath it crying! Where do you get such ideas?" But this scene would only surface years later when Lulu had a deep need to ask about the man of whom they never spoke.

Soon it was as if the first four years of Lulu's life had never happened, as if a magnanimous God had picked her up and put her in the pink house. As in make-believe, there seemed to be nothing about Charleston that she could fault. Never did she feel like an impostor when, like all the other children, she began to drawl her words, to soften the r's. Doing it with a smile was natural to a child wanting to heal herself. She put her weight on the image others had of her and optimism took over.

CHAPTER FOUR

1949

When Grandy first proposed to her daughter that she take the children south to Charleston, Penelope had said to Harry, "It feels like banishment!" During this conversation, Lulu had sat on Harry's bed, listening, knowing all too well that their mother was not an explorer. Given a menu in a restaurant, Penelope always ordered something already known. But Grandy's word was law.

Now Penelope called this lovely town to which they'd driven "Shangri-La, a gift!" Lulu had never seen her mother so happy, all but weeping with gratitude at the kindnesses of people who left their cards inviting her to cocktails, for tea "and a chance to meet your neighbors." Even a small child could see how Charleston opened her mother's beauty like a flower in the morning sun.

There was nothing beautiful about seven-year-old Lulu, no curl of hair, nor that kind of shy sweetness that gets small children and puppies picked up and loved. She ran to excess in length of everything, beginning with her height and ending with her feet. To make matters worse, Penelope was so lovely with her swept-up auburn hair—a style made popular by film stars of the 1940s—pretty enough to catch a man's eye and sufficiently clever to recognize how splendidly her handsome twelve-year-old son's looks book-ended her own.

Harry's immediate appeal was that of a self-possessed young man whose good looks were beside the point, meaning he only had to roll out of bed in the morning, run his fingers through his thick auburn hair and open his large blue eyes to appear totally at home in his skin. His composure was broken only by the tapping of a foot or a couple of fingers snapping that kept whatever rhythm was in his head. Simply put, there wasn't an ounce of self-awareness about him. The faraway look in his eyes—a strange color for eyes, this dark blue—was not as disconcerting as it would be on someone with less composure. But twelve is a lot of time to live with a woman like Penelope who'd always looked to her son as the man of the house and treated him accordingly.

Lulu was old enough at seven to notice that if you are not the pretty one, you had better get your act together. Grown-ups' eyes may go first to beauty but, if you have a great smile, are clever and quick, you can grab an eye, catch a hug, perch upon a knee. Wasn't this what fairytales were about? Didn't the youngest child always have to prove himself? It had dawned on Lulu early on that the pretty ones, like her mother, had no other act. Penelope could not sing a song, tell a joke, or walk on her hands, a small part of Lulu's ever-expanding repertoire.

With Harry in the house, the competition was stiff. And though she couldn't bring herself to hate him for his advantage, she was determined to discover his secret which began with the toilet seat that he left up, in spite of Penelope repeatedly asking him to put it down. To Lulu, his defiance said, "You're just jealous you don't have one." Clearly the business of peeing and how you went about it was important, all the more so for never being discussed; otherwise, her mother's eyes would light up for her as they did for Harry. Sometimes Harry would look up to find his little sister's gaze riveted on him. "What are you staring at?" he would ask, not unkindly, though obviously wishing her eyes wouldn't follow him as his mother's did.

Harry spent a lot of time in his bedroom with the door closed and his radio on. This left Lulu no alternative but to drop from her bedroom window onto the wall surrounding the house and edge her way the short distance to his bedroom window. Thus she came to see Harry's penis, the apparatus with which he was able to control his pee. What a remarkable device!

The advantages of owning something you could hold in your hand and direct, well, Lulu was filled with admiration and, yes, a bit of envy too. Judging from Penelope's fascination with her son, a penis was not unlike the money power Grandy wielded over their little family.

Here was something else that you weren't supposed to discuss, even though it was critical in their lives coming as it did from a distant source, a woman who could turn money on and off. Given that Penelope was the model of dependency, Lulu early on resolved to never be like her. A penis may be beyond her reach, yet Grandy had managed to do very well without one, controlling not just her own life but her daughter's as well.

Lulu practiced control in her early games of peeing into empty paint cans in vacant lots. With the exercise came an exciting feeling she didn't ever want to lose, the thrill of the forbidden. Yes, it was wrong to sit on the edge of the dock at the lake in her first summer at camp, pull aside her Girl Scout shorts and lean way back so as to pee the best arc she could into the lake, all the while trying not to wet her shorts, but if she could learn, this was all that was wanted—mastery, control!

At times Lulu feared her mother practiced the opposite of control. She had seen photos of her mother standing on a high diving board, sailing over a fence on a horse, the inscriptions below citing the dates and trophies she had won as a girl. As to where that courage had gone, Lulu figured its disappearance had something to do with the absent man in their lives: father.

Had he stolen it, or did all mothers lose their courage? Lulu was confused, given that mothers made the rules, threatening not to love you if you disobeyed. Lulu loved her mother and her teachers, all of whom were women, and she loved the mothers of her friends. Still, having your hand out all the time was scary.

On their drive south from The Dark City, Penelope had watched the four-year-old Lulu trot down the hallway of a hotel in search of the fire escape; "What a strange child," Lulu heard her mother say. But the laughter had bothered Lulu no more than it would the captain of the ship tirelessly scanning the horizon for danger. Someone had to be on guard.

If anything went wrong, Lulu surmised that Penelope with her downcast eyes would expect a prince to come save them.

Everything her mother did and ate Lulu did and ate the opposite. Had Penelope ever noticed and said something like, "No, no darling. It isn't safe to slip out of the house in the middle of the night and investigate the town," Lulu might have reconsidered her behavior. But Penelope was enmeshed in her own tragedy; what happened to others touched only superficial nerve ends, making no impression on that deep reservoir that creates a genuine emotional concern for others. She could be lovely, amusing and appealing in her neediness; but Lulu recognized that her mother became this way only when others were focused on her.

Lulu practiced survival tactics until there were practically no tests left, though it must be noted she would always be afraid alone in a dark house at night and was learning it was good to have more than one person love you. And though she disliked the unstable condition of their family life, her worst nightmare was that one of the men who came for cocktails would marry her mother and change things. What if it got worse? No, sameness was all that held their house together, sameness and Lulu's vigil of practiced control.

So she focused on the men who came to the house for drinks, casual and constant parties in this sweet, social place being very much the custom. She preferred sitting on men's laps rather than women's, a natural choice given the absent place at the dinner table where other children had a father, not to mention the way her mother went all silly around men. Lulu had no qualms about climbing aboard a man's lap and became quite successful at bringing forth smiles and small change in payment for her repertoire of jokes and songs. It wasn't surprising that men also became her models of how to be.

One man she didn't like was a certain Admiral who attended the cocktail hour more and more regularly. Surely he was the most handsome man there, an advantage of which he seemed very much aware. She had observed how beautiful women—at least those who want to have friends— pretended a friendliness to put others at ease; well, so did the Bad Admiral pose as one of the guys. Sooner or later, Lulu told herself, his ship would sail away, but the Bad Admiral was in no hurry to leave and, in time, became Chief Admiral of the Navy Yard.

Lulu was of two minds regarding the cocktail hour. That the grown-ups were merriest when smelling of bourbon and gin gave her a respite from guilt at feeling like the source of her mother's unhappiness. Downstairs their laughter rose and fell with the chorus of "South Pacific," making it sound like a party within a party, the clinking glasses in the background echoing the tympani section as the front door opened and closed to the drumbeat. Then a woman's shrill laughter would rip the scene apart causing Lulu to catch her breath until the party resumed its rhythm, assuring her of life ongoing. But much as she loved to hear her mother laugh, Lulu worried during the cocktail hour. The self-containment of the group in the drawing room below her perch on the stairway made her wonder who would take care of her if they drank too much. What if they got too merry, especially on Sundays when her mother's ever-increasing crowd of friends convened after church?

Ladies would arrive, voices hushed as a nun's chorus until handbags were tossed onto the settee, a martini put in their place, and eyes, still pious from the preaching, would look up, up at another master leaning in to light their cigarette. The past week's sins deposited at church, there was a fresh appetite, even as Lulu's own stomach growled, imagining Vangie's delicious gravy boiling down, the roast burning, the lovely white rice drying into a frazzle. From her perch, Lulu kept vigil, rice and gravy being her favorite.

Every now and then Vangie tiptoed to her mother's side and whispered, "Dinner's ready...."

"In a few minutes," Penelope replied and in that moment caught the toe of her shoe, sending her into a graceful "Whooooooops!" so that the Admiral had to catch her.

Impatient as she was for food, Lulu didn't dare leave the scene, not trusting it to hold together without her. What would have happened, for instance, if she hadn't been there the night the Admiral hit his head on a low threshold, requiring iodine from the medicine chest in the bathroom on the opposite side of Lulu's bedroom? They would never have found it if Lulu hadn't been there to help. "Don't worry, darling," the grown-ups whispered. But she did worry, her mother's gin breath making her cringe in terror. What would happen if Penelope spun out of control on gin mirth?

Lulu watched the transformation in her mother when a person in trousers, particularly the handsome Admiral, came to stand beside her. Judging from Penelope's smile and the pink flush in her face, men brought her to life. With the sleuth's keen eye, Lulu went from top to bottom on the Admiral, who was so tall he had to duck going through the broad doorways, which Vangie had pointed out were designed for ladies in hoopskirts. Because no one in her family had blond hair like the Admiral's, Lulu wondered if it were a character trait, meaning blond people were good-looking and stuck-up. But what drew Lulu's eye back again and again was the Admiral's zipper and the bulge beneath. Therein lay the clue to why her mother got so silly around him.

Harry's prestige in the family had already planted the seed of the power possessed by the penis. Lucky Harry. But The Bad Admiral's influence over Penelope convinced Lulu that what made her mother blush was the Admiral's bulge at which no one was supposed to look. It was as impolite to gaze at his magic as it was to look at the money the Admiral put on the table at the end of a restaurant dinner. Penelope actually looked away when the waiter brought the bill.

It was confounding, this business about money and the bulge in men's pants, neither of which could be discussed, though both were charged with excitement and danger. Once Lulu put a sock in the crotch of her underpants and strutted in front of a mirror though it was no more rewarding than the change she carried in her pants pocket and jingled casually as she'd seen men do it.

Things that mattered were adding up, things Lulu didn't own, not just money and a penis but also the enviable closeness of Harry and Penelope playing a duet on the piano. Harry didn't enjoy his mother's sitting next to him on the piano bench, their four hands so close that Lulu had to look away. He would sigh when his mother insisted he "scoot over so that we can play a duet." Afterwards she'd hug Harry and call him "my little prodigy."

As much as Lulu hated the union of her mother and brother, she feared even more the idea of Harry one day in the far-off future going north to some famous college. Sometimes, when their duets at the piano got to be too much, Lulu would leave the room lest she slam the lid down on their fingers and cripple them like the Phantom of the Opera.

Her own desire to play the beautiful love songs reached into the tenderest part of her. After two o'clock dinner, she would go upstairs to the drawing room and lay her fingers on the piano keys, long, strong fingers that found the chords to the love songs. Though she was a little girl who swung in trees and climbed high walls, she was drawn to the sweet meltdown of love songs, mesmerized by the illustrations on the covers of the sheet music, couples staring into one another's eyes, dancing in one another's arms, absolutely lost in love.

Sometimes when Penelope was out of the house, Harry would go to the baby grand and play his own special kind of music which his mother didn't like. "Harry, darling, must you play that loud awful jazz?" Penelope would chide when she caught him at it, softening her criticism by ruffling his hair. Shrinking from her touch, Harry would say, "You mean.... *this*....and *this*?" he would pound the chords. "Yeah, I gotta play it loud to make all that shit up north go away." After a final chord, Harry would get up from the piano and leave the house. Just where he went Lulu didn't know, but she was sure it was someplace dangerous where his music was loved and his bad memories momentarily forgotten.

The only thing Penelope hated more than Harry's jazz was the toilet seat he refused to put down after he had peed. What raised toilet seats and jazz had in common was unclear, except that Penelope sighed deeply over both.

Lulu would have liked to ask Harry if their father, The Phantom, had loved romantic music, there being so much of it—and well used at that—in the seat of the piano bench. Often enough she had left openers that might have segued into Tales of Our Father. But Harry chose to let them pass, though he often bought Lulu records of the latest "I'll die if you leave me" music. "You're such a funny kid," he would say, looking at her with real love in his eyes and then go away.

"Vangie, am I good girl or a bad girl?" Lulu would ask when the guilt inside had awakened her the night before, and her nurse would laugh and say, "You d'best little girl I know, sweet baby…. Where you get ideas like 'dat?" Lulu would look at the floor and maybe that afternoon or the next go to Woolworth and put a cardboard full of bobbie pins in her pocket when no one was looking. But giving substance to the guilt didn't help. The shoebox under her bed was full of purloined objects, absolutely useless.

Oh, how Lulu would have loved to put the box under her bed "in moth balls" as she heard the Navy men discuss ships stored away.

*   *   *

When Grandy came to visit, life in the pink house shifted into high gear. There was never much advance notice, just a phone call alerting her daughter to "keep the weekend open." Then Grandy appeared, beautiful as a movie star with her dark hair, high cheekbones, and violet eyes. Some said she resembled Rosalind Russell, but Lulu thought she looked more like Gene Tierney. Grandy had a way of walking and talking that was different from other women, a manner that said she was used to being admired and enjoyed it. There was nothing self-conscious about Grandy, an ease Lulu absolutely adored, hating the way most grown-up women looked like they were always afraid of falling overboard.

The day of Grandy's arrival, Lulu hung around the front door, determined to get the first hugs and kisses. And there was sure to be a handsome man along, someone who never took his eyes off Grandy, not like a servant but like a real close personal friend who'd shared lots of adventures with her. When at last she arrived, there was a man in tow. Lulu could see the sweet looks they exchanged, the raised eyebrow, the way he lit her cigarette and shared a slow smile.

Once they were settled in the dancing room, Grandy brought Lulu to sit beside her, as though they were a threesome, Lulu, Grandy, and the man who won Lulu's heart simply by immediately talking to her in the same voice he used with Grandy. Why can't I be their child? Lulu thought, travel with them, sit in a deck chair on board a ship going to Europe, which is what they had been describing to Lulu.

With Grandy in the house, the sad, angry feeling of being left out of the bond between her mother and brother disappeared. More than anything, Lulu wanted to be rid of the teeth-grinding hate she often felt at Harry whom she loved with all her heart. "How is that possible?" she asked Grandy in a sort of by-the-way voice, when she'd ventured to discuss it with Grandy on the second day of her visit.

"Why, Lulu darling, we always get angrier at the people we love most," Grandy answered. "You don't hate casual friends when they don't telephone. It's the people you love most who drive you crazy when they make you wait. Aren't I right, Steven?" she chided him, and Steven blushed, causing the three of them to laugh conspiratorially, which seemed to miff Penelope, Lulu noticed.

Grandy's money was as conspicuous as Penelope's lack of it; the pink house, the furniture and the paintings in it had all come from Grandy. "I'm a collector," Grandy answered Lulu's questions about the pretty paintings, "been collecting art from before you were born, sweetheart. Which is your favorite painting?"

Lulu answered, "Oh, the one in my music room. I picked it when they were unwrapping one of the crates in the basement."

"Ah, the Mary Cassatt," Grandy said. "That is, my copy of that lovely painting," and she told Lulu of her days in Europe studying art. "But alas, I'm not a good artist, so I gave it up. Before I leave, I'll give you two more paintings for your room."

Grandy had sent down so many crates, most were still not unpacked. "Just leave them there," Grandy had ordered Penelope. Sometimes Lulu went to the basement and investigated the big wooden boxes, some as tall as she and marked in bold lettering, Southampton, Genoa, Calais. The glamorous names cried to be opened and investigated, but Grandy had demanded the crates be left shut.

* * *

By this time, all those unfinished sentences and knowing looks between adults as if to signal, "Hush, not in front of the children," only fueled the fire.

Silence can be a formidable teacher. The rules governing the hush-hush attitude about money and sexual parts were teaching Lulu to listen for what was left unsaid and to watch where the eyes went. When it was clear that no good deed would get her mother to see her as beloved, Lulu's eight-year-old mind bargained, "Very well. If you won't see me, I will not live by your rules regarding money and the badness of my body."

Clearly the avoidance of the cost of things was a girl thing. Men discussed money as if it were a game and they looked straight at you when they talked about it, instead of staring at the floor. As sure as two nickels made a dime, Lulu understood that her mother's focus on Grandy had to do with money. It seemed that everyone was drawn to Grandy because of her ease and, Lulu was sure, that ease came from the coins in her purse. On this understanding Lulu built her determination to gain the essential element of Grandy's power: She too would be "easy in her skin"—Grandy's expression—would pay her own way, never be dependent like Penelope.

That Penelope never noticed Lulu's need for new dresses, that hems were out, sashes gone missing, was a fact of Lulu's life. She made do without complaint. Every now and then, Harry would buy her something pretty; it would just appear on her bed in its paper bag. When Lulu tried to thank him, he'd smile and say something like, "It's okay, kiddo." Though she knew where Harry got his extra cash for his presents, she was too mindful of his privacy to admit she'd followed him several times to that place where he played the piano.

CHAPTER FIVE

1952

Lulu's favorite place to visit was what she called "The Secret Mansion." The day after they'd arrived in Charleston five years ago she had seen the wall beneath her bedroom window and decided to drop onto it. The old walls ran behind and alongside the houses in this, the oldest part of Charleston. The wall was high but close to the house and wide enough to carefully follow, using the overhead branches for balance, best done barefoot. Soon she had come to a juncture of neighboring walls that offered a kind of platform comfortable enough for her to lie on her stomach and peer down through the limbs braided together.

"My tree house, just like Alice in Wonderland" she had thought when a parting of branches revealed her first glimpse of The Mansion, an enormous old building with shacks strewn over the property, all crumbling and softened by the years so that the broken masonry, shutters hanging askew, roof and chimney more sagging than suggesting majesty, loaned it an otherworldliness.

"The people who live there don't care about the broken parts," Lulu had thought approvingly. Chickens and dogs ran in and out of The Mansion's many doors and windows from a yard so vast Lulu couldn't see where it ended. The rusty pieces of metal sheeting over broken windows, a tin "RC Cola!" sign blocking a doorway, old iceboxes and rubber tires from every size vehicle…why, all this "found stuff" looked to Lulu like the treasures of an industrious people.

Smoke was coming from the main chimney that first day Lulu stared down as Gulliver might have, and while the people weren't Lilliputian— many in fact enormous in size and spirit to match—they were wonderfully individuated in look, sound, and activity. The small children, dozens it seemed, were clothed in the same old fabric that covered masonry holes and frameless windows, a nice design it seemed to Lulu. Then, abruptly from inside the pink house had come Vangie's voice. Lulu, her dress dirty and torn, Mary Janes missing, arms and legs scratched, had worked her way back home. But from that time on, when no one was looking, she'd been out her window and along the walls to that place where she could lie on her stomach and watch the life below, wonderfully different from the world she inhabited, not just because of the color of the people's skin— though it mattered deeply, being in Lulu's eyes the source of their amazing energy. What also made them special was that they touched and laughed a lot.

Lulu kept a blanket and a pillow in her tree house so that she might more comfortably watch the games of Red Rover in the yard below, or watch a big Momma tending her babies on the second floor veranda that wrapped The Mansion. A long parade of high arched doors opened onto this "piazza," as Vangie called it, and though some of the doors hung by a single hinge, Lulu found it the most beautiful place she'd ever seen.

A good distance from The Mansion was a shack to which everyone sooner or later paid a visit and stayed a while. Since its visitors sometimes carried comic books or newspapers, Lulu concluded it was a kind of reading room, a supposition set straight one day when a little boy ran from the shanty bare-bottomed and followed by his mama who wiped his bottom. An outhouse was a fascinating idea to Lulu who occasionally enjoyed a pee in the high grass.

As Lulu turned five, then seven, then nine, she still went to her tree house to watch the people in The Mansion. In the evenings, she was often privy to lovers' trysts, a boy and girl kissing and touching, Lulu holding her breath lest a grown-up round the corner and discover them, the boy's hands in the most surprising places, and the girl near falling down. Lying on her stomach atop a bed of tangled branches and vines, softened by a thick mattress of fallen leaves, Lulu came to appreciate the exciting tension that near-discovery brought to the lovers. Lessons were being learned, a foundation laid for the later preference for forbidden men and their dangerous desires, rule-breaking already her favorite form of fun. Oh yes, she could understand the thrill of stealing kisses. Hadn't she tasted the added succulence of stolen Snickers?

One evening she'd leaned too far forward and fell, a slow motion descent, most of it through a mountain of leaves, decades of foliage banked against the high wall on the property line and up into the lower branches of her tree. Because Lulu could hear people's voices coming ever closer to where she lay buried, she wasn't afraid and called out, "Hey, it's only me, over here...."

Everyone in the yard ran to see what had fallen from the sky and landed in the two-story-high pile of leaves. "Bring me 'dat chile, y'all heah? Bring her t' me!" a grandmother yelled.

So high were the branches and leaves, it required three grown men forming a human ladder to reach Lulu, all the while the Grandma hollering for them to hurry. Soon enough Lulu was brought to the old lady who rocked her in her arms, warm and round as the breast against which Lulu lay. Seeing up close for the first time the people she'd been watching for so long, Lulu smiled, calling two of the children by name. "Tyrone, Betty Lou, did y'all know I was up there in my tree house?"

The children doubled over in laughter that Lulu knew their names. "You gotta' name, honey?" an old man asked.

"Lulu," she said, and everyone repeated it, tasted it, all the while touching her gently. From far across the wall she could hear Vangie hollering for her. "I better go home," she said. Hands reached out to brush her off and a little girl asked, "Lulu, you gonna come back?"

"Oh, yes!" And she did. Some nights she'd climb out her bedroom window and go there to sleep for part of the night. Several ladders had been joined together securely atop the mountain of leaves. Other nights she'd take the safer route and walk around the corner, down the narrow alley and through the high brush that hid The Mansion from the world. So genuine were the smiles when she arrived, Lulu came to believe they really wanted her. In the early morning someone woke her to get her home before breakfast, though Lulu was sure Vangie knew all the while.

There was neither electricity nor modern plumbing in The Mansion. Like the other children, Lulu slept in her underwear and when she had to pee went barefoot down the hall to where there was a bucket. She didn't much like getting her feet wet, though nothing dampened her image of life in this house where the sounds of people making love, a baby's cries, the drunk arguments and laughter were teaching her that good and bad things happen in a family and it stays together. Nothing could keep her from returning. Her visits filled a need as instinctual as an animal licking its wounds.

Not only did these people love her but in their midst she felt "seen," which was the only way she could describe it to herself, a proof that she was flesh and blood and not like "The Shadow" on the radio program. With Penelope, well, there was nothing she could accomplish, no prize at school, no athletic award, not even the badge for selling the most rat poison door-to-door when they'd had a plague in the historic district of town. As for the people at the Mansion, whose eyes really did light up when she appeared, well, they saw her all right, saw her and, yes, loved what they saw. But the secretiveness of The Mansion was what Lulu loved most, there being no entry to it, unless you knew the dirt path off the unpaved narrow alley.

Then came a day when ten-year-old Lulu was contemplating whether to go down to the waterfront and rummage through the abandoned railroad cars, or to steal some old linens from the closet upstairs and take them to her tree house. She was sitting in the drawing room, her idle fingers playing across the drawers and doors of her mother's desk, when, as she raised her feet to allow Vangie to mop the tiled floor, a small door sprung open at the back of the desk revealing a stash of letters held together by a rubber band. Only then did she notice the tiny key which was not usually there.

Lulu looked quickly over her shoulder to be sure Vangie was out of the room, then put her hand into the dark well. There was a letter, a long narrow envelope with her mother's typewritten name on the outside, and a return address from The Dark City. She removed the rubber band, opened the letter and began to read. Had someone at this moment put a restraining hand on her shoulder and asked what she was doing, she would have answered in all innocence, "I don't know. I just had to do it."

But no one asked and so she read. The letter was from a doctor at Meechum Memorial State Hospital, its name in big type at the top of the front page.

May 12, 1946
Dear Mrs. Templeton:

I regret to let you know that your husband Charles Stanhope Templeton's condition has not improved.

As you know he is suffering from a severe manic depressive psychosis. He has had two rounds of electric shock treatments without any noticeable improvement.

However, the main reason I am writing to you at this time is that after your last visit your husband had a severe manic episode. During this he attacked nurses, doctors, and other patients. He had to be restrained, given heavy doses of sedation, put in a camisole, and isolated.

In view of the above, I think it would be wise for you not to visit again unless you hear from me.

Sincerely,
Dr. Harold Battleberry, M.D.
Director of Psychiatric Services

Lulu's lips silently formed the syllables of her father's name. What is a camisole? My father is in a place for crazy people, she thought, imagining scenes of insane asylums remembered from movies. They'd always scared her and now she knew why. The sound of Vangie approaching, singing an island spiritual, alerted Lulu to fold the letter, return it to the secret compartment, close the door. Shazam, as in the movies, the door clicked. She turned the tiny key as well, but was betting it wouldn't be there the next day. Or had her mother meant her to see it? "No, Lulu!" she scolded herself. Now Vangie shuffled into the room, stopped at Lulu's chair and said, "What's my little gal up to? I knows you, Lulu Templeton. Vangie can see d'wheels movin' in dat little head." Lulu didn't respond, and Vangie shuffled out the door, picking up her hymn where she'd left off.

Why did I always tell people he was dead? Lulu wondered. Someone along the way must have told her to say it. Now the secret was hers to keep. Oh, she wanted to do the right thing! "Should she go to him? Bring him to Charleston where everyone gets well? Why had mother left him there?? Lulu bowed her head over her clasped hands. "Dear God, please tell me how to help my father. Give me a sign, God, like in the Bible. I could run away and go to him…or make myself forget what I just read." Abruptly Lulu's fingers, restlessly roving around the desk, unintentionally re-opened the little door. "Oh, it must be a sign! I will write to him," she instructed herself. "Tell him I will come for him when I'm big enough."

"Why you lips movin?" said Vangie, rounding the corner once again. "You talkin' to yourself like d' lady in 'Gaslight.'"

"Tomorrow," Lulu said to the compartment.

But the next day the compartment was locked, the tiny key gone.

CHAPTER SIX
Later in 1953

It wasn't that Lulu was unaware of the midnight noises down the hall, but as long as Vangie was in the room next to her she had slept with them. Familiar and loved was the muffled sound of Harry's radio which he kept under his pillow while he slept. Even though Harry kept the volume turned down low, Lulu's ears picked up the saxophone, sometimes Dinah Washington's wail of despair. Eventually she had woven these sounds into her dreamsleep, imagining her brother sitting on the edge of his bed, smoking his cigarettes in the dark, his foot moving with the beat. Behind him on the wall was an enormous old poster he'd found in a junk store, on it a black man coming down a long flight of stairs, playing a trumpet against a background of fiery red on which was lettered in black and white, "Jazzé moi, bébé!" In the lower right-hand corner was the date, Paris, June 1936.

Then, shortly after Lulu's tenth birthday, Vangie had announced that she would be sleeping at her own home. "You a big girl now," Vangie had said, and Lulu felt the safety of childhood go out the door with her nurse's bundles. Now the noises of the old house became more demanding. She was accustomed to the sounds of her mother's life on the floor below, the piano, the phonograph music, a particularly loud burst of laughter. Now with Vangie gone, Lulu was even more alert to what happened in the pink house, including her mother's footsteps on the creaky stairway late at night when she came to say goodnight to her son, all in keeping with her rapt attentiveness to him.

Ever since reading the letter from her father's hospital Lulu had been having nightmares too hard to handle. One scary night after Vangie had moved out, she padded down the hallway to Harry's room seeking sanctuary. "Harry?" she whispered, and, when no answer came, she began to climb in bed behind him. But someone else was already there, the perfume familiar. Mother! Making no further sound, Lulu backed out of the room.

Thus was the forbidden made real, a familial S-curve, one body folded into another, innocent enough once upon a nursery but full of portent when a grown son lies with his mother's body tucked into him from behind like a spoon. Backing away from the scene on cat's paws, Lulu closed the door silently and sank to a small heap on the floor. Tucked into her misery was fear for Harry: "Who would save him?" But just as powerful as her fear was her grief and the saddest loneliness. "Nobody wants me," her lips formed the words spoken to the crack beneath the door.

Eventually she padded back to her bed and slept. From that night on, she would lie in her bed and listen, praying her mother wouldn't come. But no matter how late the evening downstairs ended, Penelope would finish the night in her son's bed. Anticipating the footfalls on the squeaky stairs, Lulu would hold her breath until the fourteenth tread, followed by the discernible click of the door handle opening and closing Harry's door. Lulu would grind her teeth until her jaw ached, or put the pillow over her head and focus on the games she captained at school.

Sometimes when sleep refused to come, Lulu would tiptoe down the hall, and put her ear to Harry's door. More than once she heard her mother's hushed voice, "Harry, dear, won't you put your arms around me? I'm so lonely. You used to love to lie on my breast, don't you remember?" But Harry said nothing.

One night Lulu opened the door without a sound—a technique she'd practiced to perfection when no one else was home—and just looked at them, Harry facing the wall, his mother tucked in behind him, her arm across his shoulder.

Lulu's feelings ran from abject loneliness to rage, then to the terror felt when she'd read the letter from her father's hospital. She had to be very careful not to become like her father, she warned herself.

Before sleep that night came the thoughts: Why hadn't mother found a better hiding place for the letter from her father's hospital? Why wasn't there a bed big enough for Lulu to be with her and Harry? Didn't Penelope *want* her? She was only eleven…but she'd have found a place for that letter that *no one* would discover! She wished she'd never seen it!

Sometimes she just curled in a ball on the floor outside the door, nursing her grief at being left out of the family dyad, an ageless wound. In her mind's green eye, Harry and Penelope became a template of what she would never allow herself to see or feel again: a man she loved in the arms of another woman. In Lulu's eleven-year-old soul, this promise didn't negate her love of Harry, merely complicated it, as only siblings can twist and turn upon one another.

Then things began to happen very fast, beginning with the night the police came to The Mansion next door, the sirens and a woman's screams waking Lulu. Quickly she was out the window, moving barefoot along the wall until she reached the tree house. Below, all the kerosene lamps in the mansion were lit and the police were taking away a woman while the others wailed hysterically. A stretcher was brought and a man's body was carried out the dirt path leading to the alley.

Early the next morning, Lulu hurried to The Mansion which was unnaturally quiet. One of the children whispered to her that Esther had found her husband with another woman and killed him. "Killed him!" Lulu repeated. For the first time she felt out of place at The Mansion and returned home to find Vangie rocking back and forth, weeping over the dishwater in the kitchen. "Esther find him with 'dat woman and she do what a woman gotta do. He betray her!"

Lulu had seen murder in the movies, but that was Hollywood. So, real people did it too! She felt relieved, of just what she wasn't sure, except it was comforting to know that other people were worse than she. One thing was sure: falling in love was dangerous.

Lulu sat on the stairs listening to Penelope discuss the murder on the phone. "Those people are uncivilized," Penelope was saying with disgust. Lulu disagreed. "Oh no, I'd kill someone if they took Grandy or my best friend Fanny away from me."

Now Lulu had an action and a word "betrayal" to put with the buried feelings inside. She didn't believe black people were different from white people. It was just that white people kept everything inside.

A few months after Harry's fourteenth birthday, he must have been waiting for his mother outside his bedroom door because the first thing Lulu heard was Harry's voice in the hallway. "No, mother," he said sternly, followed by a muffled reply from Penelope. Quickly, Lulu was out of bed and in Vangie's old bedroom that adjoined her own. Here she lurked at the door opened slightly to the hall, listening and watching through the crack.

"Harry, darling, I won't sleep if I can't lie beside you," her mother's littlest voice implored.

"I'm too old for this, mother."

"A son is never too old to let his poor mother...."

"I've had a new lock put on the door. I'm going to lock it now so, unless you want to wake Lulu, go back downstairs."

Lulu dared not move until Harry had closed, then locked his door. Penelope stood weeping, beseeching her son to let her in. Finally she descended the stairs to her own room. Only then did Lulu return to her bed where thoughts raced like the tickertape in Times Square that she'd seen in newsreels when the war ended. It's over, she thought, and slept the most grateful sleep.

Several weeks later when it seemed clear that Penelope had given up her visitations to the third floor, Lulu was awakened by another noise, something outside her bedroom window open to the warm summer air. Someone was moving along the high garden wall that ran alongside their house just below the third floor windows where she and Harry slept, a wall that Lulu assumed was her own private walkway to her tree house or an escape by which she could drop via tree limbs and adjoining walls until she reached the street. Charleston contained a grid of these ancient brick walls and now someone or something was out there. It was Harry. She reached for jeans and a shirt, counting on Harry requiring more time than she to work the walls. Once he had reached ground level, she concluded, he'd be going for his bicycle behind the house. By the time he had wheeled his bike out front, Lulu was on the ground waiting.

"No, Lulu, go back...." Harry urged.

"I'm coming with you! If you say no, I'll follow you anyway. Oh please, Harry, don't leave me out. I can keep a secret better than anyone!"

"Oh, God...just stay close behind me."

"This is my favorite time to see Charleston. I'm not afraid!"

"You've been out alone before tonight? Okay, but let me go first and, when we get there, stay back until I motion you to come." Harry smiled at her in his heart-breaking way. "What a kid you are."

"Oh Harry, our first adventure together!"

"Let's hope it's not the last, kiddo. Ready? Remember, stay a little distance behind...just in case."

And off they went, single file, the whirring of the bicycle wheels on the slick pavement the only sound hanging in the night air, until the deep bull horn of a ship somewhere out to sea reminded Lulu to take an even deeper breath of the sweet salt air. So loaded was the night with portent that neither of them spoke. Then the clouds parted and the moon smiled down, like in a Disney movie, Lulu was thinking; she was happier than she'd ever been, sharing an adventure with Harry. They didn't pass a single soul as he led them along the waterfront, past the elegant antebellum houses and closed shops, until eventually they reached Blacktown. Here Harry made a wide, slow curve to the right where the asphalt ended. On the grassy empty lot close to the water's edge stood a wooden shack— well, much larger than a shack, Lulu thought. What with the red and blue light bulbs and the loud music inside seeming to make the walls expand and retract, it resembled something out of a Disney movie.

Harry stood by his bike, seemingly checking the tires until Lulu made the turn and pulled up alongside him. "I can't take you inside," he said, "because there's a lot of drinking and, well, they wouldn't understand."

"I'll just watch through that window at the back. Harry, this is the most exciting thing that's ever happened to me!"

"Okay, but stay back there. I'll tell these guys to keep an eye on you." Harry walked over to one of the bouncers and explained the situation. "My little sister had to see the action. Do me a favor and look after her." The man nodded affably, slapped Harry on the back, and smiled back at

Lulu who was already at her position, lost in the shadows by the window with the best view inside.

It was better than a movie. Without panes in the window, Lulu didn't miss a beat of the music nor a syllable of the many cries of rapture from the audience as in, "Oh, baby, you on fire!," "Sway me, Harry, go man 'n break m' heart!," all this as soon as Harry sat at the piano, joining the men on trumpet, saxophone, and a very, very old man playing the drums with the frenzy of a twenty-year-old.

The pig-tailed face watching from the deck outside was lit with rapture, the patrons indoors oblivious until the excitement overtook her and Lulu was yelling and moaning with the wildest when Harry and the saxophonist finished "Round Midnight." People were standing on their chairs, bobbing and weaving as in a Holy Roller ceremony, while some couples couldn't resist the dance and were glued to one another in bliss, pressing their bodies together as if it were the Day of Judgment. Then the mood changed as Harry swung into Ellington's "Take the A Train."

Lulu stared in awe at her brother, never before having heard him play this way, flat-out, mind and body at one with the rickety old piano. Then she looked closely around the room, wanting to remember the faces, some streaked with tears, others lost in bliss, eyes closed and many just shaking their heads like it was unbelievable.

But the climax of the evening was when a beautiful black girl silenced the room by simply walking across it and up to Harry's piano where she stood behind him, back to back, seeming to lean up against him, her hands pressed to his sides as she sang "The Man I Love." Being a child of the movies and a lover of love songs, Lulu understood instantly Harry's burning necessity to get out of the pink house and ride to this place. From the minute the tall, graceful girl ran the palms of her hands down Harry's body and sang from deep within "Some day he'll come along…" well, Lulu knew from watching them that he'd come along, and that Harry was more madly in love than all the men in the movies put together.

CHAPTER SEVEN

1953

Harry had the blues. He hadn't played the baby grand for over a week. Making music was what fed him, an intravenous feeding that was electric to watch. Now there was no juice, hadn't been any for eight days. Lulu feared that he would lie on his bed in that room, smoking cigarettes, staring into space, until he withered.

Penelope had given up trying to coerce him to the dinner table. "He won't starve," she said with resignation. But Lulu wasn't so sure; Harry didn't even listen to the jazz on his radio. Never before had his room been silent.

Problem-solving was a challenge Lulu couldn't resist. Her deep love for Harry along with her inkling of the source of his misery represented an opportunity. It had all begun when Harry stopped playing piano at The Hot Spot a week ago. By this time Lulu had discovered the beautiful black girl's name, Stella. There had been an argument between one of Stella's brothers and Harry, though Lulu was certain it went back to Stella's mother who also didn't like Harry. Having witnessed the electricity between Harry and Stella when she sang, draped over his piano, Lulu could grasp how separation from such a feeling could give a guy, the blues.

Something had to be done, and Lulu knew just who had to do it. Harry and Stella needed a secret place to meet. Lulu took up the quest; if there was a chord of revenge on Penelope for leaving her out of her nocturnal trysts with Harry, so be it. Revenge was becoming a familiar emotion for Lulu.

One afternoon, she packed up leftovers from the two o'clock dinner to take to Flossy and her cats, and on the sly slipped out the back door taking the route through the neighbors' gardens and over the wall to the abandoned house where Flossy lived. This house with its fractured sunbeams full of sprites and mites sliding through the old shutters across the wide-beamed floors—this would be a fine meeting place for Harry and Stella.

She would show them several out-of-the-way routes to approach the house just in case one wasn't safe on a particular day. Before telling Harry, she would do a little decorating, steal some blankets and pillows from home for a sofa, some orange crates from the grocer so that there would be a table for candles and plates. Oh yes, when friends get together and talk privately, its important there be baloney sandwiches and cookies. Penelope's cocktail parties had taught her the niceties.

When Lulu offered her plan to Harry, walked him through the various approaches to the house, the boards across the windows promising privacy, Harry had beamed at Lulu so warmly that she blushed. "Thank you, little sister," he said. "Some day I'll pay you back."

"That's all right," she demurred, warmed to the bone.

Lulu had four days before the lovers met. Through Flossy, who was on the floor below, she found an extra mattress in a closet on the top floor; it was old and dusty but, once dragged down the stairs and covered in clean blankets and pillows squirreled out of Penelope's linen closet late at night, it was, in Lulu's appraisal, "not bad, not bad at all."

Because the windows were boarded over, some form of light would be needed. Penelope preferred candlelight when she was entertaining, meaning the silver candlesticks from the cupboard below her mother's sideboard had to be polished. But how? "Oh Vangie," Lulu asked, "shall I help you polish that fruit bowl on the dinner table?" and, when the job was done, the silver polish was pocketed, along with ivory candles, linen napkins, and a selection of magazines to put on the orange crates.

The night before the tryst, Lulu emptied the refrigerator. "I'm having a party in my secret hideaway," she told Vangie.

"Uh-huh," the black woman said.

Appraising her work, Lulu was especially proud of the small cake she had decorated with Necco Wafers. Rather than ruin the effect, she even talked herself out of a sample.

At the last minute she couldn't resist waiting on the other side of the party-wall to enjoy their pleasure. But when first Harry and then Stella arrived, they didn't notice the cake. They fell into each other's arms, stripping off their clothes so quickly that Lulu was sure they'd be so wrinkled Stella's mother would be suspicious. The kissing overtook them, all balance lost as they staggered, buckled at the knees, fell upon each other onto the mattress. Then Harry rose on his haunches like Neptune out of the sea, staring down at Stella for a moment until—what is this? It's his weenie blown up three times its size! Nothing now could have torn Lulu away. She was no longer a witness, but a bewitched participant. It was like watching an enormous snake going into a tiny hole, an impossibility you might think. But Gulp! the snake slipped readily inside Stella who obviously wasn't minding it at all, even though she was moaning and crying out.

"She likes it!" Lulu told herself. A revelation, even a benchmark in Lulu's career.

It was all happening so fast, the lovers' dance both edifying and remarkable given the pictures it imprinted in Lulu's imagination, seeds of forbidden fantasies all the more thrilling for sending Penelope's rules up in flames.

On and on the dance went, pulling Lulu's eye, by way of the chink in the wall, into the very center of the erotic storm. Round and round their legs and arms slipped and slid, wet with body juices from him, from her, until drained, drugged, though still not done, Harry moved down her body, buried his face between her legs and began to eat her like a juicy peach, his tongue amazingly long and pink, licking that place that was supposed to be vile. Because Harry found it delicious and Stella enjoyed having it eaten, it would never be vile again.

Lulu was breathing heavily, forehead and hands dripping wet, not unlike the lovers who had begun to moan and pant, clearly the end of the race in sight for Harry once again was pumping faster and faster into Stella who called out, "Oh, baby, don't stop, don't stop!" and then they began to cry out together. "Oh, God, oh yes, yes, yes!" And Harry threw back his head, made a deep guttural sound, and collapsed on top of Stella.

For a few moments all was so quiet that Lulu tried not to breathe. Her chest heaved sympathetically for the exhausted athletes who were slowly beginning to rub their wet bodies together. In one graceful movement, Stella rolled them over, and she lay on top of Harry, driblets of her sweat falling like rain onto him. "Oh, baby, baby, what you do to me!" she sighed. They slept.

From her side of the wall, Lulu readjusted her position, her forehead sore from being pressed against the wall; she had bitten her bottom lip which was bleeding a bit, and her legs were asleep from her awkward crouch. But she dared not move, her role as guardian, and as voyeur, impressed upon her. She felt no embarrassment at having witnessed what she now realized to be something, well, religious. And the more she thought of it, keeping watch over Harry and Stella asleep in one another's arms, the more akin it became to the scene in *The Brothers Grimm*, where the fairy godmother watches over Hansel and Gretel asleep in the forest.

Lulu's eyes ran up and down the length of Stella's beautiful body, as tall as Harry, one long arm paired with his, the underside of her hand cradling Harry's "thingy," the most delicate pink color Lulu had ever seen. So matched were their intertwined bodies, Lulu understood why Harry just had to be with her.

After the lovers had awakened, put on their clothes and left, Lulu and Flossy ate the pound cake. "I have to get some real sheets next time…and maybe mama's portable radio, some nice music," Lulu told Flossy. The old black woman transferred the cake from her hand onto the mattress where they sat, and she took Lulu's two hands in hers, turning them palm up. Lulu stared at the old woman's bandannaed head bent over her palms as Flossy's breath heated, then rubbed them together until they felt like they were on fire, which was when Flossy spit on them, clapping them together like cymbals, chanting something in a language stranger than Gullah.

"What did you say, Flossy?" Lulu whispered.

"You be safe now," Flossy said in a tired, satisfied voice. Then she stretched her bony legs, ashen grey like the rest of her, and smiled, the grey-blue lips spread ear to ear in a toothless grin. "What you see 'dis day, Lulu, not a bad 'ting. Not bad a'tall. Folks tell you it bad, 'dey jus' jealous. You 'member what Flossy say."

* * *

There wouldn't be another picnic for Harry and Stella. A few days later, Penelope ordered Lulu to go to her room, saying she had to speak privately to Harry. Naturally, Lulu closed her door upstairs loudly, then tiptoed to the top of the stairs where she could not be seen. The drawing room below occupied most of the second floor, meaning there were no doors to keep Lulu from hearing everything.

"I received an unwelcome call this morning from your, uh, friend Stella's mother," Penelope spat the words, unable to even get through her opening sentence with her intended equanimity. From here on, she was pure witch. "She is pregnant and determined to have your baby, you little idiot!" Penelope paused only long enough to reload. "How could you do this to me?" she roared.

"It wasn't aimed at you, mother. Stella and I are in love. I'm glad she's pregnant. You see, she didn't want to marry me. Now maybe she will."

"And you with a brilliant musical career ahead of you. She'll drag you down, she'll...."

All this Lulu heard from atop the stairs, though Penelope's screams could have been heard from anywhere in the house. Lulu was terrified that her family, small as it was, would be blown even further apart. She moved closer to the banister, grabbing the posts with all her might. "No, Harry, don't say it..." she prayed to herself, even as his words were being formed.

"Shut up, mother. We'll be out of town before word of this leaks. I'm going to marry Stella. I don't want to hurt you, but...."

"Hurt me?" Penelope shrieked, "you've destroyed our family just when we'd got away from what happened up north, built a new life. I could kill you!"

Lulu heard scuffling noises and Harry yelling at his mother, "Put that down...."

Terrified that the murder at The Mansion would be repeated in her own family, Lulu came down the stairs to see Harry wresting a heavy brass candlestick from Penelope, who fell sobbing to the floor. "You're only fifteen, Harry…you don't have to marry…."

"How do I get this through to you, mother? I want the baby, I want Stella…."

"Sweetheart, after all we've been through together, after your father… why, without you…."

"This isn't about you!"

"Oh, isn't it?" and now Penelope's voice was icy cold. "You…you want to marry a Negro…." She hissed the word out like a snake. "…A Negro! Why, no decent family would have the two of you!" When Penelope saw that he was turning from her, walking towards the door, she cried out, "Oh, Harry, my sweet Harry, I'm sorry, I'm sorry…."

But Harry was unmoved. From where Lulu sat, halfway down the stairs, she saw that her brother had grown visibly taller, and the register of his voice had dropped as when someone assumes a higher responsibility.

"I'm going upstairs to pack a suitcase," said Harry. "You've always treated me like the man in the family. Don't treat me like a child now. I'm going to marry Stella. We're leaving for San Francisco tonight."

So fast had the drama escalated that Lulu was in shock at what she was hearing, that is, until the word "tonight." Not tonight! No, Harry couldn't leave tonight! She couldn't' live in this house without him, the only sure thing that held her life together. The tears coursing down her face, Lulu hadn't seen Harry move to the stairs. He reached down and took her two hands in his.

"Your hands are cold and wet, Lulu," he said in the dearest voice she'd ever heard, and pulled her to her feet. For a minute he held her against him, saying in her ear, "I need you to help me now. We have a long life together, little sister. I promise. Now, come with me while I pack."

From behind them Penelope's voice railed on. "She's black, do you hear me? Black! If you go with her, I'll report you. The police will pick you up…."

Harry stopped. "If you try to stop us, mother, I'll start up with an even blacker girl and I'll make sure the whole town knows."

Penelope's tone took another tack. "Very well, you're clearly your father's son. You'll need money. I'll go to the bank tomorrow."

Harry half-turned to his mother on the landing below. "I think it best we leave tonight," he said, and Lulu's tangled thinking went to the play they'd seen last week at The Little Theatre, a play called "The Letter" in which a woman suddenly goes from hysterical to killer control, and shoots a man dead on a stairway just like theirs.

"Stella and I leave tonight," Harry repeated in his new grown-up voice. He turned from his mother and, with his arm around Lulu's shoulder, walked her up the last flight of stairs and into his bedroom. He set her on the bed, both hands on her shoulders, and squatted in front of her. "Look at me, Lulu. That's my brave sister. Now, I'm going to pack and, while I do, you and I are going to talk like this is just a trip, meaning I'm going to write more letters than you could ever read, okay? And I'll telephone and send you pictures. Oh, Lulu, please don't cry...."

She tried to stop, which took a bit of doing given the anguish at the thought of their house without him. "Let me help," she said and folded clothes as Harry handed them to her. When the packing was done, the suitcase closed, Harry moved to the door. Lulu quickly blocked his way.

"Tell me about him, Harry," said Lulu. "Give me a picture of him." Lulu's voice had lost the supplicant's tone. She was cool, all little-girl sadness turned to iron determination.

Harry's mouth opened in protest, then perhaps he realized it was the one gift he could give and long overdue at that. He put down the suitcase, walked them back to the bed, and sat. "Oh, God, I promised mother to never...but, no, you deserve this. Come, sit next to me." All gentleness now, he brought her down beside him.

"Mother's put so many bricks around him, it's like an archeological dig, but here goes. My best memory of our father. I only had time alone with him once, when mother was pregnant with you and went to Boston to be with Grandy until you were born. It was the best time of my life. He took me everywhere, hardly ever left the house without bathing me, dressing me, something he'd never done before....

"'This is our secret, son,' he'd say, winking, standing beside me in front of the tall mirror in his bedroom. Talking to me in the mirror he'd say, 'This is our adventure while your mom's away.' And so I put away those wonderful days with him, burying them to please him and to protect mother. I was only four, but he took me everywhere: restaurants, his club, the racetrack where he gave me money to bet. We'd go to the paddock. The jocks all knew him. He was so sweet, not just handsome and generous, but deep down sweet....'"

"Like you, Harry," Lulu whispered, her eyes intent on him, so lost was she in these pictures he was painting, pictures for which she had been starved, a glimpse of the father she'd been missing all her life, a void she'd tried to fill from scraps grown-ups inadvertently dropped. But in the end, the efforts were unsuccessful, the void of him more substantial than real life. Every little girl had a father but her. Even one lost in the war left pictures behind and memories. Now she was getting the transfusion she'd always needed, yes, literally, his blood, or so it felt, Harry's movies of him making her more alive than she'd ever felt. When Harry started to stand, she grabbed his hand, pulled him back down beside her. "More!" she said.

It wasn't lost on Harry what he was providing. "Okay, here's my favorite memory. We were in a nightclub, the band playing conga music, you know, 'One, two, three, la conga!' and a woman slipped and fell down. Before she could get embarrassed, dad fell down, too, intentionally. Even a little kid like me could tell he did it to divert attention away from her. Know what everybody did? They all fell down in a heap, one, two, three, la conga! That became our secret after mom came home, this little conga step. Mother would say, 'What's that all about?' and he'd just wink at me."

Lulu had been smiling at the pictures Harry painted but now, her head bowed, she stared at her hands folded in her lap, and asked in a small voice, "And when Penelope came back home with me...?"

"You know, I don't remember her being pregnant, just dad talking about the baby that was coming, telling me how much I'd love you, said it was the only thing he'd ever ask of me, that I take care of you. When he got the phone call that a baby girl had been born, he turned to me and said, 'Shall we call her Lulu, like in the song?' Right from the start he made you something I was part of. You were our baby. We'd go shopping to buy you pretty things. He planted that in me, that I would love you like he did. My secret time with him, my favorite time." Harry stood. "I have to go now, I really do...."

Lulu grabbed his arm. "Please, Harry, just one more picture. You don't know how much...."

"Okay, okay." Harry closed his eyes. "Once he took you and me to see Grandy. 'Don't tell your mother, son,' he made me promise, like it was an adventure. He really loved being bad, y'know? Even back then, Lu, Grandy just couldn't take her eyes off you. Dad was so easy and open around her. Well, everybody was...and he and mother weren't getting along well those days. So it was great to be with him and you and Grandy and everyone having a great time. I remember he gave the camera to Grandy's butler to take a picture of the four of us, and then Grandy took one of Dad and me holding you...."

"I bet Grandy liked him. She likes good-looking men who make her laugh...not like the Bad Admiral."

Harry looked at his watch, then at Lulu whose face was a mask of grief. He pulled her to him and spoke quietly. "This is like trying to remember another lifetime, Lulu. Okay, before he went in the Army, some days when mother was busy he'd pick me up at school, he'd be out there, the hood down on the car, and he'd holler, 'Hey, Harry my boy!' and all the little kids would turn and see this guy waving at me, his hat pushed back on his head, y'know, like Clark Gable, and I'd run down the steps outside the school and jump in the car." Harry paused. "Maybe I made this up and it never happened, but, no, it was real all right, the realest thing in my life. It's just that everything in our lives is so hushed up we're not even allowed to think about him."

Harry grabbed his suitcase and turned to go, but Lulu was ahead of him, her back to the door. She had forgotten to ask for an essential piece of the portrait, and Harry must not escape before filling it in. She said, "If you tell me real slow exactly how he looked, then I'll always have it."

Harry closed his eyes. "He didn't look like anyone else," Harry said. "Tall, thick dark hair, black eyebrows to match. Lots of mischief in his face, high cheekbones, full lips, like you. And when he went off to war, even I went all shy when I saw him in uniform, he was that handsome. Got the picture?"

"Got it." She opened the door but stayed close to him as he walked to the top of the stairs. When he was halfway down the stairs, she hurried after him. "But Harry…." He hesitated, then continued down, until she caught his sleeve and said, soto voce, "…and there wasn't a terrible scene when I was under the dining room table, a fight and blood all over a man's face…?"

Harry stared at her, standing one step below, his eyes full of question and fear. "I don't know what you're talking about."

"After the war, when he came home, before we came to Charleston. He couldn't' just disappear, Harry."

"He was a hero, got a medal." He looked at his watch. "I've got to go. Stella's waiting for me." He took Lulu's arms from around him, kissed her tear-stained cheeks, went down the stairs and out the front door.

A deranged Penelope's last words echoed as the door slammed. "Harry, you can't leave! You're the prince!"

Lulu stood frozen on the stairs, trying to take in what had just happened, not just Harry's leaving but the hole it left inside. Is this what men do, walk out on you, first Daddy and then Harry? And she promised herself: "If anyone leaves when I grow up, it will be me."

In the days following Harry's departure, Lulu came to accept it was a good thing he'd left; otherwise, Penelope would surely have killed either him or Stella. Until now Lulu had been reluctant to see her mother clearly, needing to believe she was a potential source of love even if it wasn't yet available. But now the portrait fractured and past instances of Penelope's meanness surfaced: whispered conversations on the telephone reporting the transgressions of women friends who'd strayed from husbands, or a woman who'd betrayed another woman's confidences.

Lulu was old enough to recognize betrayal, having known it herself among her friends when little girls put their heads together and whispered nasty things about another girl, close as kin until the irresistible urge to leave another out. No wonder, Lulu thought, mother doesn't recognize how evil the Bad Admiral is. Adults only see what they want to see.

* * *

Ten days later, Lulu got a letter postmarked Albuquerque, New Mexico. The postman was about to put it through the mail slot in the front door when he saw her walking home from school. "Oh, thank you, thank you!" Lulu exclaimed, recognizing Harry's handwriting. Her first thought was gratitude that Penelope hadn't seen it first, for she surely would have opened it, no word having yet arrived from Harry by telephone. Lulu raced to her room, closed the door, and climbed out the window onto the wall which she walked until she'd reached her tree house. Now she opened Harry's letter, the first she'd ever received from anyone except Grandy.

August 1953

Braveheart,
The escape from Charleston was a horror movie, but I'm
glad we had that talk about our father. I wish I'd told you
sooner. Now that he's out in the open, ask me anything.

We're still on the road, heading west. The first few days were
the toughest. The Burma Shave ads—like the ones we saw
long ago driving south to Charleston—make me think of you,
but sometimes the highway gets lonely and kind of scary. Last
night some rednecks surrounded our car at a filling station in
Alabama. They looked at me and Stella and got as furious as
Mama. I tell you, Lu, the prejudice fills me with so much sor-
row for Stella, but she's tough. I know we'll make it.

We did manage to spend one night in a cheap motel that
would take Stella and me—some black GIs just back from
Korea demanded rooms for themselves and us—but mostly
we sleep in the car. At night we pick up the Moondog, Alan
Freed, from radio station WJW in Cleveland, just as I did in

*my bedroom in Charleston. White kids, thousands of us across
the country, listening to black music. That's the future.*

I'll write again as soon as we get to San Francisco.

Remember I love you,
Harry

Lulu thought of reading Harry's letter to Penelope, not that she wanted
to share it with anyone, but she worried about her mother who had con-
fined herself to her bedroom since her son left. From the doorway Lulu
had seen Penelope lie in the rumpled sheets. Long ago she had heard
Penelope confide to a woman friend, "I'd never have got through the sad
events up north without my son. He was always my little soldier. Some
day I always dreamed he'd find a sweet, compliant, southern girl who'd fit
him just fine."

Then one day when Grandy telephoned, Lulu told her of Harry's flight
and of Penelope's solitary mourning in her bedroom.

"Go in there and tell her to pick up the phone by her bed!" Grandy
ordered Lulu who tiptoed into her mother's room, picked up the phone,
and whispered, "Grandy wants to talk to you, mama." Penelope groaned
so audibly Lulu was afraid Grandy would hear. "Please, mama, take the
phone" Lulu hurried from the room so as to miss nothing when she got
to the extension in the drawing room.

"Listen, daughter," Grandy was ordering Penelope, "you get out of bed
and take care of your other responsibility, namely Lulu. This is no time
to neglect...."

"A fine example of motherhood *you* are!" Penelope wailed, which was
the first time Lulu had ever heard her talk back to Grandy.

"Get up, get dressed, or that Admiral of yours will think you're no
longer interested and take up with another woman!" And Grandy's words
had the desired effect. No sooner was the phone hung up than Lulu heard
her mother running a bath.

CHAPTER EIGHT

Now, no one sat at the piano, so Lulu did. Long ago she'd promised herself to do nothing her mother and Harry did. Now there was this irresistible song in her head. Her foot on the soft pedal so that Penelope wouldn't hear, Lulu picked out the notes of "My Foolish Heart," a song from a movie that touched deep inside. Because it was "their" music, Harry's and Penelope's, she'd forbidden herself to investigate the sheet music in the piano bench. But it was also "his," daddy's! With Harry gone, the rules changed and Lulu lifted the lid of the bench, picked up the old sheet music one by one, and read the song titles. "You Made Me Love You," "I Surrender, Dear," "What Am I Gonna' Do About You?" "If I loved you," "Love Me or Leave Me," "Body and Soul…." Oh, and the pictures on the covers of men and women in each other's arms, dancing, kissing, dying of love. Wonderful!

Emboldened by the sheer number of people all over the world who were clearly like her, dying for love, Lulu sat and spread her long fingers across the keys, feeling the fullness of a love song, singing it softly as her father once had, his fingers moving over the tops of the silent keys.

Tears of lost love were about to spill, when the telephone rang. Penelope answered in her room and, hearing Grandy's name, Lulu picked up the drawing room extension. "For God's sake, stop boo-hooing!" Grandy was saying. "Your son impregnates a black girl, runs off to California, and you're still crying? Listen, Penelope, and mind what I say: Another unwanted pregnancy in this family and I'll send all of you back up north where the climate will cool your blood. That Admiral's on the make! You uncross those legs of yours…worse yet, ever allow Lulu to…. Shut up, daughter! She *is* your responsibility. I'll put her in boarding school and you on the street if you slip up once more!"

"Don't call my son a 'slip up!' He's a wonderful boy…"

"That's not the point. Dear Lord, doesn't this family respond to anything but sex and money?"

"You can't order me around like a child," Penelope wailed. There was a pause, until a very calm Grandy said, "Pay your own way, Penelope, and you can be mistress of your fate."

Before Grandy could hang up, Penelope begged for more funds. Grandy refused. "I don't know what you do with all the checks I send. That's what comes from never having made a penny yourself."

"Mother, after what you did, don't you think you owe me…?"

"I owe you nothing." Grandy hung up.

Worried how her mother was bearing up, Lulu went upstairs to find Penelope, looking like a little girl lost, the receiver still in her hand. Sensing her mother wanted to be alone, and feeling a rare pity for her, Lulu decided to pick her some flowers from the neighbor's garden.

Lulu went to bed that night trying to piece together what sex and money had in common. Thoughts of the Hot Box and The Mansion came to mind, places where people knew how to live life, laughing, dancing and, yes, the sex word too. Sex is what got Harry in trouble, Lulu thought, but it didn't look like trouble when I saw him and Stella doing it at Flossy's house. They were having the best time…like it was something they never wanted to live without. Clearly sex and money were so important no one talks about them. The thought was so revolutionary Lulu wrote it down and put the paper in the secret compartment of her new wallet.

Before turning out the light, she wrote to Harry:

> *I've been so lonely for you, Harry, but I had an idea, something you*
> *and I could do together. My secret mansion, the big old house below*
> *my tree house, well, that would be a great place for us to stage a*
> *musical. We could write songs together about life in the Mansion. Ev-*

erything happens there. I'll write lyrics and you can write the music. There's a fight going on right now between two families in the house, sort of like Romeo and Juliet where they don't want their kids to be in love. But they are in love! I'll write a poem and send it to you. Then you can write the music. What do you think, Harry? Please say yes!

I miss you and love you, Lulu

P.S. I just got braces on my teeth. I look like Frankenstein, but I'm learning to wrap my upper lip over my teeth when I smile so people can't see all the steel.

CHAPTER NINE
1953

Lulu lay on the wrought iron balcony outside the drawing room, reading for the fourth time Harry's letter from San Francisco, paragraphs of excitement that meant he'd probably never come back to Charleston. Harry said there were Chinese people, and Japanese, and that the jazz was even wilder than the Hot Spot or anything he'd ever heard on the radio! He was waiting tables but he'd already got his "big break" when the regular pianist at a joint called The Black Hawk didn't turn up and Harry had to take his place. "It was just one night, but I didn't embarrass myself." He and Stella had an apartment and everyone spoke some crazy language where men were called "cats" and women "chicks" and "stoned" was being high on something you smoked called "pot." Everyone was "hip," "cool," and "groovy."

"Grooviest" of all, Harry wrote, was her idea of the blues opera based on the Mansion next door, something they could write together. Oh, he really loves my idea! Lulu thought, and wants me to make up a story, send him descriptions of the characters. Best of all, Harry enclosed a piece of music he'd written, "just for you, Lulu."

She pressed the pages to her face to see if they smelled of the other ocean. What was "pot?" Was "The Black Hawk" the place Harry still played piano? Oh, Harry, must you be so happy out there? She'd been hoping the letter would say he was coming home. On the stamp was a picture of the Golden Gate Bridge, and with the letter came photos of Harry and Stella on a street with Chinese people.

Also in the envelope were two pages of sheet music with Harry's scrawl on the top of the first, "The Secret Mansion" or "Lost Charleston." Lulu began to pick out the notes on the piano, wishing she could play with both hands. In despair, she returned to the balcony. "Oh, I'm such a stupid girl not to have taken more lessons!" she whispered.

"Hey up there," a male voice called. Looking down, Lulu saw a man on a motorcycle wearing jeans and a pair of aviator glasses turned to focus on her. "You must be Lulu," he said, removing the glasses and rolling the bike backwards, the better to take her in via eyes so green she could see their color from where she stood. The man and his machine seemed to fill the landscape beneath her, the pastel colored houses across the street all but dwarfed in the shadow he cast. Then he swung one leg over the monster bike and began rolling it toward the wrought iron gate. "Shall I put it back here?" he called.

"Oh, yes. Please, come in. I mean, don't go away, wait for me. I'm coming down!"

There he was when she opened the door, standing in front of her, filling every space. His jeans were tucked into cowboy boots and he wore a leather jacket like fighter pilots wore in the movies, but it was his deeply tanned face, the blond hair falling in his eyes from beneath the leather helmet he wore, that movie star face with a movie star smile that froze Lulu. For once in her life she was speechless.

"I guess Grandy didn't tell you I was coming," he said. "I'm Marcello." He held out his hand, his eyes never leaving hers, and she took his hand and closed her mouth, thinking that he must be used to people staring for he seemed to have all the time in the world and the nicest manners, too.

"If you are the real Lulu and not an impostor," he said, "then I'm your uncle. Your mama's mother, Grandy, married my dad. Get it? Now, can I park my Harley or shall I go on to Savannah?"

"Oh, no, you'd hate Savannah!" Lulu whipped into action, ready to throw herself in the way of his leaving. She ran to the side gate, opened it and stood back, the better to see him. "Are you really my uncle?"

"Forever and ever, bella," he said softly.

"Bella?" she asked in a small voice.

"Bella means pretty."

"My mother's pretty, but I...."

"I'll be the judge of that," he said. "What say I put it all together and call you Lulubelle? Now, where's the bathroom? I've been on the road since...hey, ever been to Myrtle Beach? No? We'll drive up some weekend, just you and me."

Worried he might never reappear, Lulu stood sentinel outside the bathroom. When the door did open, he was no less amazing than at first sight. Feeling the heat in her face, she reached for his hand and led him upstairs to the drawing room. "I'll make you something cold to drink," she offered. "A gin and tonic." She made the drink from memory, having watched the grown-ups often enough. Above all else, she must keep this man, charm him. "How about a cigarette?" she asked, reaching for the box on the coffee table.

"No, the drink's fine," he replied and crossed to the piano, took the glass from her and said, "Thank you. Now, shall I play you one of my favorite tunes? It suits you perfectly," and he struck a few chords and began to sing "Younger Than Springtime." Stopping only long enough to down the gin and tonic, he went into "Out Of My Dreams and Into Your Arms."

"You like love songs, don't you, Lulubelle?"

"Oh, yes! They're so...."

"I know. Me too. I bet you play the piano like a dream."

"Oh, no! Mother plays and my brother Harry. But I know all the words to all the songs. You, though, you sing better than the people on records."

"That's how I earn my bread and butter."

"You mean Broadway?"

"No, movies, probably ones you've never seen, and nightclubs. I grew up in Hollywood. My daddy was a bit player, so he and Grandy enrolled me at MGM."

"Metro Goldwyn Mayer? You went to school there?" Incredulity overtook shyness.

"Went to school, had a few small parts, then left. Couldn't take the life. So I went on the road, me and my three girls, my back-up singers. We do nightclubs, hotels. Some day I'll show you my staircase. That's how I enter, at the top of the stairs, spotlight…! Hey, I'm talking all about me and it's you I want to hear about."

"No, please. Let's sing another show song." Then she remembered Harry's letter. "Better still, my brother Harry sent me a song he wrote. It would be great if you'd play it for me." She ran to the balcony and came back with the song Harry had sent. "See, it says 'Lulu's Lullaby.'" She put it in front of him.

Marcello leaned forward to better read the music and sang:

"When I dream of Lulu,

I see her as she was

When we were young…"

Lulu was not prepared for the beauty of his voice matched with Harry's words and music written just for her. The tears spilled just as Penelope entered the room. Marcello, all in one movement, stood, kissed Lulu's wet cheek. "We'll finish this lovely song later…" and embraced Penelope.

"March, sweet March, my long lost brother…whatever brought you down here?" Penelope was laughing, genuinely excited for the first time since Harry's departure.

Lulu fell back, a bolt of jealousy draining all joy from her. But consummate performer that he was, Marcello freed one arm to include her, drawing her close to him.

"Penelope, you never told me you had a lovely songbird for a daughter…."

"Oh, you mean Lulu. Well…" Penelope patted her daughter's head already even with her own and uncharacteristically reached to smooth the hair come loose from her braids. Lulu ducked away from her mother's hand. "Come, let's have a drink." Penelope turned back to Marcello. "Tell me how long you're staying."

Lulu sat on the piano bench, watching and listening, absolutely sure she'd never seen her mother so at ease and happy. In the conversation she again learned that he was a half-brother to Penelope.

"But what brought you all the way down to Charleston…?" Penelope asked.

"Had a date at a club in Raleigh. Grandy mentioned on the phone Harry leaving town, said you were having a hard time dealing with it…."

"Oh, March, you came all the way down here just to see me…?"

"There was a time you and I were close, remember? Living in that house with Grandy, you were the only one who took my side…"

"How could I not? You're my little brother. Once upon a time it was you and I against the world, which is how I see Grandy…"

"By the way, what is it with these shipments coming in from abroad? What's the old lady up to now?"

"Oh, it's just stuff she collected in Europe after the war. It's stored in the basement. You know mother and her 'collections'…cares more about them than any of us, except for Lulu, of course…."

"Why don't I hang around for a few weeks, cheer you up? By the way, Grandy mentioned a certain evil Admiral…."

"She resents anything good that happens to me! Well, I'm not giving up the Admiral!"

"That'a girl! Come on now, show me where I've got to stay."

Not until she'd heard Marcello agree to stay "at least for a little while" in the old converted cookhouse out back did Lulu feel it safe to leave. For the first time she believed there were ways, besides the beauty her mother owned, to catch a man. After all, didn't she and Marcello both love romantic music? Maybe he would teach her to read music better so Harry could send her his songs for their Blues Opera. What a nice man, she thought to herself, coming all the way down to see them because they were so sad without Harry.

* * *

The day Marcello moved into the cookhouse, everything changed. He took on the grief over Harry's departure as his own burden, promising to check up on Harry through his West Coast connections. Whenever his half-sister got close to tears, he would divert her with other family tragedies that had turned out well. Soon the rigidity went out of Penelope's shoulders and a trace of playfulness took the place of her need to control everything and everyone. Marcello delighted and amused her friends, his arm around his sister so as to include her in the aura of Hollywood he brought with him. Simply put, he gave of himself tirelessly, as though there were no limits to what he could accomplish for this household that had been in mourning since Harry left.

But Lulu knew she had his heart. Sure of his love and grateful for it, she could soon watch him with her mother and feel no resentment. Hadn't he promised that the two of them were just alike? And when she confided in him her shame at being jealous of Harry, he'd explained that it was natural. "Your hottest jealousies are for the people you love most and are afraid of losing to someone else," an incredible idea at first but full of sense when she thought of her life.

It wasn't lost on Lulu that Marcello and Penelope's conversations were full of the mysterious past, incidents and family members of whom Lulu only knew the scantiest details. Whenever she heard their voices in the drawing room, she'd tiptoe down to the step above the stairway curve where she could hear and not be seen. Though today was baseball practice, she chose to stay and listen. Marcello was the only person in whom her mother confided.

"I've not spent time with Grandy in three years," March was saying. "We talk now and then when she wants a favor done. Never known anyone like our mother...."

"I've not seen her in ages," Penelope sighed so heavily Lulu cringed, hating it when her mother pulled these pitiful sounds from deep inside.

"Grandy moved us down here for the children's sake, or so she said." Penelope went on, "But she has business here. These shipments that arrive, much of it her own work, paintings she stored in Europe at the end of the war."

"But why store them here?" Marcello asked.

"God knows. But she ordered me to have a platform built in the basement in case of rain, flood, whatever...and keep them here 'until further notice.' Our mother," Penelope sighed. "If it weren't for Harry and Lulu,

I'd never hear from her. Of course, she dotes on Lulu, sees herself in all that independence and scholarship. My Harry…" and here Penelope's voice got all wobbly, "well, she already imagines Harry at Carnegie Hall. Oh, my brilliant son…. No, no, let me finish. For a moment I'd forgotten he's gone, taken that black girl with him.…"

Before Penelope could give way to grief, Marcello knelt in front of her, his arms around her, Penelope once again in such misery that Lulu felt her own tears coming.

"Shhh, we'll sort this out, I promise," Marcello said. "At the very least I'll meet with Harry when I get back to the Coast. Trust me. You always did in the past, remember?"

"You were wonderful when Grandy made me sign poor Charlie into that place. But if I hadn't, she'd have turned her back on us. I'd be penniless. We certainly wouldn't be in this lovely house."

So there it was, out in the open, confirmation by her mother and Marcello that her father was in "that place." The hidden letter she'd been trying to dismiss was made real. Now in Lulu's mind's eye was a picture of Penelope signing him into a crazy house and then running away, taking the key with her. Wouldn't he be waiting to be saved by his youngest child, as it was told in movies and fairy tales? Was this her task, to find and free him? Or maybe the test was about knowing the secret and keeping it hidden, a test of obedience and silence. Besides, what could I do? Lulu asked the critical inner voice. She was only eleven and she had no money to go and see him. But the inner voice sneered: The real hero in the tale is always poor! That's what makes him heroic. He surpasses all expectations! I could ask Marcello about him. But if I lose his love I'll be alone again. I must be calm and not go crazy like my poor father. Grandy thinks I'm a good girl, loves me. She doesn't want questions from me. Can I live with the secret, keep my knowing from them? Yes! I'll keep the secret even if it eats a hole in me! I'll put it with the other secrets. If I ask about him, we might lose this lovely house like mother said and be banished from Charleston. I'll bury it deeper than ever this time. I'll swallow three times and it will be down, forgotten: One, two, three! But I *will* find him!

* * *

In the days ahead, Charleston, given its love of eccentrics, took Marcello to its heart. He learned the Gullah chant of the shrimp lady who rolled her cart every morning past the pink house. His baritone would echo her singsong, "Ah be deedle floun', de roe, roe, shrimp!" and he would appear in moments on the sidewalk, as in a stage entrance, to buy her wares.

The white linen suit was welcomed everywhere. Well-traveled, cultured, and with beautiful manners, he was soon indispensable at any dinner party. And he repaid the many kindnesses with a talent it seemed for almost everything.

At the local theatre's casting for "The Lady's Not For Burning," he won the lead. Hearing that The Daughters of the Confederacy required something appropriate as backdrop for General Wade Hampton's Anniversary, Marcello painted a vast canvas of Hampton's historic meeting with Lee at Gettysburg. He'd located a vacant warehouse on the waterfront where he designed an enormous studio upstairs, covering the floors with faded Orientals. He moved in a grand piano, easels and enough old drapes and shawls to decorate a variety of shabby sofas and chaises lounges so that he and his new friends might spend evenings reading plays aloud, listening to music, and falling in love.

Penelope gave him several of the paintings from one of the crates in the basement. They were unframed canvasses depicting a street scene, a dance hall, and a still life. "God, they're really good," Marcello exclaimed. "I knew she'd studied painting when she lived in Paris before the war, but I never realized Grandy was so talented."

"Don't tell her I loaned you these. There are so many, she'll never miss them. Our mother seems to have a special vendetta with each of us. Our family's more like the court of Louis XIV than a real family." You and she getting along better?" Penelope asked. "What is it between you two?"

"Remember years ago when she went to Pamplona with Bertrand? I was thirteen. I was sitting at the piano and saw them coming up the lawn, both in white with red sashes they'd worn at the running of the bulls. Grandy introduced him, then went upstairs. Bertrand seduced me.

It wasn't hard. 'Open your mouth when you kiss,' he said which is when mother walked in. She sent me back to Hollywood, to the studio school. Never much wanted me around again."

"Never wanted any of us around," Penelope added with bitterness. "Of course, it's different with Lulu."

"She's a great kid, Penelope. I'm teaching her to paint, to dance, to think better of herself. I'll play Pygmalion…no, I mean it. Such a sweet, mixed-up kid. I'm crazy about her."

"Be careful. She'll fall in love with you."

"I hope she does. This one's heart I won't break. Don't look so skeptical," March laughed. "I'm no Saint Francis of Assisi. I've never met anyone tailor-made for what I have to give. A girl who needs a musician on a motorcycle. I'm really glad I came down here. For the first time in my life, I really feel like I'm part of a family."

Lulu stowed away this overheard conversation, like a treasure.

* * *

"Only to you do I give this, Lulubelle," he announced formally one day, placing a key to the studio in her hand.

Every day from then on she walked to the waterfront, carrying the key. Unlocking the small door on the ground floor, she climbed the wooden steps to the vast space of his studio, high as the church behind her house and dark as night save for the skinny threads of sunlight that skipped in between the boards that made up the two enormous doors through which cargo had once been loaded into the warehouse. Lifting the wooden slab out of its cradle, she pushed one wooden door and then the other, stepping back against the onslaught of sunlight overwhelming the place with such force, the brightness felt like a tidal wave, racing past her, around corners, filling empty wine bottles carelessly left the night before so that they shone like a candle had been lit inside.

Yet it wasn't just light brought inside but the sounds from the harbor, seagulls, a ship's horn, and the occasional holler from a longshoreman. Lulu would inhale the sea air, along with and from behind the potpourri of the night before, March's cologne, the wine, booze, cigarette and cigar smoke from the group he'd brought from the little theatre.

Today she took her notebook and sat in the archway, remembering last night when they'd read aloud "The Cherry Orchard" and an opera called "La Boheme" was playing. She'd fallen asleep and was waking up when she heard them closing the doors. Someone had said, "Poor girl, she's asleep," and she'd feigned a near-death sleep so that Marcello might carry her home.

"What should I write about?" she said aloud, looking at the blank page in her lap. "Write about something you feel deeply," Marcello had said. And she had answered him honestly, the only person she trusted, "You mean, write about the evil Lulu?" and he had pulled her to him. "My little girl, what am I going to do with you?" he'd asked and then added soberly, "If you are to be a writer, you must own your fear, use it as ink. Then it will be yours and you not its."

Now Lulu's eyes went to the wharves where a boat captain was arguing with a laborer. Into the picture walked an old couple she knew from Helen Street. They were taking an afternoon stroll. What is it like to be old? Lulu wondered, imagining all the years between them and her meager eleven. And then it came to her what she knew best, her fearsome jealousy of her brother and mother's relationship that closed her out, and the terrible rage it provoked. Lulu began to write.

* * *

Watching Marcello with his friends at the warehouse, Lulu was impressed by what she called his "constancy." He never slipped out of character. Yet, one night she'd seen him grab hold of a guy who'd humiliated a woman and half-carry him by the back of his shirt down the steps and out the door. But that, too, was "in character." No, you wouldn't want to rub Marcello the wrong way. He talked to men and women with the same concentration, not with his eyes wandering around the room, and when another person's remarks really registered he lit up.

Of course there were a few people Marcello really, really liked, one a very handsome dark-haired man from Atlanta and the other a woman who'd flown in from Las Vegas, just to see him. The woman was staying at March's studio, and the dark-haired man would come from across the room like a B29 and walk between them when they got too close.

Lulu understood that Marcello made love to these people, maybe right here on the chaise where she sat, but after all, hadn't he told her that what they had was more special than any other relationship?

She and March had seen a movie where Gene Tierney lets her husband's little brother drown, sits in the rowboat and watches him sink beneath the water even as he begs her to save him. After the movie March had said to her over their chocolate nut sundaes, "Jealousy's the meanest emotion in all of life. That's why you and I, who know we really love each other, will never let jealousy get to the killer stage. Okay?" And she had agreed, which is how she came to live easily with the way women and men looked at Marcello. "Go ahead, feast your eyes," she told them silently during the evenings on the waterfront. "He's mine."

CHAPTER TEN

1953

It was one of their outings, one for which they'd waited so that the
moon would be full and they could sleep under the stars, that a terrible
thing happened that turned out to be a blessing. Marcello had a destina-
tion in mind, a point of land heavy with oak trees and surrounded on
three sides by water. "All the better to see our lady of the moon enjoy-
ing her reflection," he had said, strapping their sleeping bags onto the
Harley. They'd ridden past Charleston's many churches, past the great
park where battles of the Civil War had been fought, the original canons
still intact, then they had crossed the narrow bridge over one of the city's
two rivers connecting with the Atlantic Ocean. On the far side of the
bridge they stopped at a grocer's in Blacktown and picked up staples, fresh
bread, fruit, cheeses sniffed carefully by Marcello who raised an eyebrow
at Lulu's insistence they include peanut butter. "How can I take you to El
Morocco if you refuse to eat caviar?" he asked, putting several jars of the
little black eggs in his pocket.

A mile beyond the city limits, they took a left onto a narrow and rut-
ted dirt road. "See why I told you to wear jeans?" he hollered over his
shoulder, and Lulu put her arms tighter around him, burying her face in
the smell of him. The brush on either side was dense with brambles and
wild flowers fighting for the light; the long black vines hung downward
from the trees, tough ropes of creepers that had plaited themselves into an
almost impenetrable curtain. Every once in a while a shaft of midday sun

would break through and Lulu would catch a glimpse of a shack on stilts, bits and pieces of laundry hanging on a line.

"Did you see that house, March? The door was painted blue to keep out the evil spirits."

"We like spirits, right?" he hollered back. "Keep an eye out for anything moving over to the left."

Soon enough she caught a glimpse through the foliage of a man loping along on a mule. "There, there!" she hollered and March put two fingers in his mouth and whistled. The mule's head parted the gray curtain of moss, and Lulu could see that the man's bare feet almost touched the ground. He rode bareback, an old rope for reins, and behind him strapped on the mule was a bundle of sugar cane.

It would always seem to her that March's exchange with the man had been rehearsed, so smoothly did the meeting run, a settlement reached wherein they followed the mule and the man to a shack constructed of boards and nailed-together license plates. Rusty metal advertisements for aspirin and cigarettes along with gunnysacks of grain on the front porch signified that the shanty was a store. The dark interior offered the fresh shrimp and oysters that March had anticipated.

Lulu shook her head when he offered her an oyster. "What am I going to do with you? These are the best oysters in the world." To prove the point he ate several right there, prompting an exchange of words between him and the delighted store owner.

"Where'd you learn to speak Gullah?" Lulu asked when they were back on the road. "I've never heard a white man talk to island people like you."

"Leave a little mystery in life, bella. Another five minutes and we're there."

True to his word, they came to a point of land seemingly scooped out of the rugged coastline. It was as if the trees and foliage behind them had agreeably decided to hold back at this point and arrange themselves in such a way as to announce this gentle piece of land and the loveliest prospect onto the blue glass water that emptied into the ocean beyond.

"How did you find this?" Lulu exclaimed, eyes full of joy and wonder, not just at the idyllic beauty of the place, but at his ability to once again make magic. "Did you create it? I thought I knew all the lovely secret places, but this, this…let's never leave! You and I, we don't need the rest of the world!"

Lulu unrolled the sleeping bags under a giant oak, and then changed into dry clothes. She watched Marcello diving and floating in the water. "Sacred water," the black man had called this place, the exact spot where the Holy Rollers held their baptisms. This is the happiest day of my life, she thought, watching him.

"Come!" March held out his hand. "Come stand on my shoulders and dive."

"No! You'll see how big my feet are!"

He laughed aloud. "What is it with you women and feet? Long feet are proof of a good dancer. Come on, Lulubelle, spread your arms wide like a swan and dive…. Good girl! Well done…. Let's go deeper, I'll race you….."

Every so often he'd retreat to the beach and put another record on the portable phonograph. Mary Martin and Ezio Pinza's voices wafted across the water where Marcello and Lulu danced in one another's arms, she so light in the salty water that he could hold and lift her until they both fell, out of breath, laughing.

"Will you teach me to dance, I mean, on dry land, March?"

"You're born to dance. It's written all over you. But sure, I'll teach you to dance and to paint and anything else you want."

They lay on the beach, so close she could feel the hair on his arm, maybe the sweetest feeling she'd ever known. He rolled on to his side and brushed with his fingertips the hair that had dried on her forehead. "Spending a day with you is a gift," he said, "I can feel how sweet it is being eleven and free."

"Me, a gift? Gosh…how do you mean, you weren't free?"

"Grandy enrolled me at Metro before I was five." He stood. "Here's the best thing I learned at Metro Goldwyn Mayer." March did a perfect backward somersault.

"How much older are you than I?"

"Twelve years, a lifetime. Oh, I'd give anything to be your age. Never had eleven, was always twenty-four going on fifty. Tell you what, I'll teach you all the tricks I learned when I was young and you'll be the generous Lulu who lets me into her world. Deal? Now I'm going to show you how to build a fire."

He was beautiful, a word she'd only heard used for women up to now. The hair on his chest was dark, unlike the thick blond hair that kept falling in his dark blue eyes. And his legs, well, she'd never noticed men's legs before, but March's were long and muscular, the wet hair on them…but she cut herself off. "He'll think I'm stupid," she said to herself.

He was telling her the story of Lancelot and Guinevere when Lulu excused herself to find a secluded spot to pee. When she finished and was burying the Kleenex with which she had wiped herself, she saw the dark spots. Unsure where they had originated, she inserted another Kleenex on her index finger up her vagina. There it was again, a dark spot, not red like blood but brownish. What was it? Did the holes get confused, poop coming out the front? Suddenly scared, she looked to where Marcello lay, hands behind his head, staring at the heavens. Don't be embarrassed, she chided herself, March loves you! Ashen and full of shame, she approached. He saw her face, and stood.

"What happened? Did a snake bite you? What have you got in your hand? No, give it to me." He took it, opened the wadded Kleenex and looked from it to her. "What is this? Where did you get it?"

Lulu put her hand between her legs and pointed up. "There, up there."

"Oh, sweet girl! How wonderful! Don't you know what this is?" He put it to his nose. "Yes, yes absolutely. Lulubelle, you have begun to menstruate. How perfect to have it happen *here*!"

"No, no, I'm too young! Oh, and Marcello, you smelled it!" Lulu's face was red and full of anguish. None of her friends had yet begun to menstruate and she, far less big-breasted, had to be the first. It was unfair and unwanted because it linked her to Penelope, whose blue and white box of Kotex up till now signaled Lulu's separation from her.

"I'm only eleven! I hate this happening!"

His arms were around her. "I think this is just the biggest magic, so right it should happen here by the sacred waters and with someone who loves you."

"I don't want to talk to mother about this!"

"Talk to me. I'll explain how it works. We'll buy everything you need at the drugstore when we get home. But Lulu," he cupped her chin, holding her head up so that their eyes met, "there is nothing in life more magical than what happened here."

Lulu stared into his grey-blue eyes. "I'll try to believe you."

"For years to come, when you get what other girls call 'the curse' you'll think of tonight and say to yourself, 'It's not a curse at all.' I can't believe my sister didn't prepare you. Never mind, I'm the beneficiary."

"My stomach hurts. Ouch. You promise this won't change how you love me?"

"This night can't get any better. Here, lie beside me and I'll make you something." He used his handkerchief and soft leather belt to devise a comfortable enough apparatus. For her first cramps he gave her wine which soothed, making her sleepy.

"I'll remember this all my life, and so will you," he said. "The gods set in motion that you would come of age with someone who honors magic."

Eyes closed, mind free-floating, Lulu said, "I should have been a boy."

"Because you're so brave?"

"Because I'm bad. You're smiling, I can tell. But I hide my badness so no one can see. Sometimes my evil feelings wake me up at night."

"Tell me where you hide your so-called badness"

"In a box inside me. Sometimes the lid comes off and it's terrifying!"

"Is this about pushing the kittens off the porch?"

"You remembered what I told you!" She sat up, thrilled that he had taken her seriously. "Mother left me behind, March! She'd packed daddy's brushes and combs and books, put them in a big hamper in the car. She took Harry and not me. I sat on the porch with my kittens and when they drove by me and didn't even look at me or wave, I pushed the kittens off the porch and killed them."

"Remember what I said last time? Kittens land on their feet. You didn't kill them."

"Now Harry's gone too...."

"Not because of you, Lulu."

"Are you sure? I don't hate Harry. I love him."

"Shhh. Sleep, little girl."

That night's full moon shone down upon them, an unlikely couple, she a girl on the cusp of adolescence, and he a musician on a motorcycle. Because of him she would have less aversion than most women to the seemingly unsightly trappings of menstruation, and there would never be a beginning of her cycle that did not return her to him, and to their shared belief in magic.

And because of her, Marcello felt something he'd never owned, a good opinion of himself. Things had come to him too easily, too soon, not always a gift. The envious eyes of others had made him uncomfortably aware of his own lack of gratitude for what he had. How could this young girl know that all the things he would like to do for her were for himself too? "Never mind," he told himself. "Enjoy it, Marcello. Take it in."

* * *

The day after the outing with March to the island, Lulu stood on the baseball diamond, aware of the boys' eyes as she uncharacteristically walked three players in a row. Until now she'd been able to separate rejection at dancing class from her role as a star on the playing field. But the ugly pad between her legs demanded precedence along with the steel on her teeth. Life was all of a piece, including this new chapter where boys' eyes glided past her, they as naturally awakened to beauty as she was to Joe, he perfectly matched to Lulu's best friend Fanny.

"I hate what is happening," she thought and the tears stung. She threw the ball to another girl and walked off the field. Without a backward glance, she got on her bike and headed for home. Taking the back door, she hoped to get upstairs before anyone saw her. But two steps up she heard Penelope talking on the phone with Grandy. Marcello was on the dining room extension, so Lulu went to the phone in the kitchen.

"Listen, mother," he interrupted Penelope, "one of you must talk to

Lulu about Charlie, yes, the whole family saga. Too many women, and Harry too, have tripped on sex, more out of ignorance than...."

"I don't want to hear this!" Penelope wailed. "It's bad enough having Lulu..."

"Shut up," Grandy ordered, followed by a wail from Penelope who could be heard running to her room and slamming the door.

March's voice dropped, as when one is telling a secret. "You've got to tell Lulu the whole sordid story, Grandy, which won't be sordid at all when *you* tell it."

"She's too young to know. It will distort her entire life... March, she's only eleven!"

"Your exact age when you first got pregnant and Penelope not much older. How can you tell Lulu, 'Sex is a beautiful thing' and not include her family...?"

"All right, all right!" Grandy sighed, then sighed again. "Sooner than later, Lulu must hear about her father, and I should be the one to tell her. Penelope would make it sound like a nightmare..." and in a small voice Grandy added, "which it was, God knows, which it was."

Shaken, Lulu quietly hung up the phone, not because she didn't want to hear more but for the first time here was a mystery she was afraid to solve. To herself she said, "Something really bad happened. Something that has to do with this thing between my legs."

CHAPTER ELEVEN

From the floor above, Lulu heard her grandmother arrive and she silently descended to the curve in the stairs where she could hear any conversation.

"Just thought I'd drop by," Grandy announced to Marcello who'd been playing the piano in the drawing room.

"I just left your studio," Grandy said. "That's a lovely portrait of Lulu you're painting. It's nice to have someone who binds us. It's good you love the child because she's totally ignored by Penelope."

Eager to see as well as hear, Lulu took a risk and rounded the bend in the stairs.

"If you've come to ask a favor on Lulu's part, she's already got my heart. Nothing to do with either you or Penelope."

"Actually, I've something else on my mind." Pacing her lines, Grady crossed to the chaise lounge, patted it, then sat on the edge. She looked very much like a movie star to Lulu as she took a cigarette from her bag and held it until Marcello crossed to her, and lit it.

"I've a number of valuables, paintings primarily, arriving from Europe by ship," Grandy went on. "After the war it's been a buyer's market and I've done quite well."

Now Grandy looked straight at March, weighing the words. Grandy wasn't used to asking favors. "I'd like you to be my contact, my go-between...." The ash of the cigarette had grown long and without an ashtray or an offer on her son's part to provide one, Grandy was forced to cup her doe-skinned glove to accommodate the ash. "…like you to be my intermediary with the Captain in charge of the harbor. There are sculptures as well as paintings, part of the Somerset Maugham collection.It will be the last shipment, as the basement in Penelope's house where I've stored the crates is quite full."

"Why not a warehouse?"

"Safer at the house."

"Is this why you sent her and the children down here?"

When Grandy ignored his question, Marcello continued, "What is precisely my role in all this, mother?"

"Shall we cut to the heart of it? The Admiral, that despicable man Penelope sees, I don't trust him."

"You think he'll steal your art collection…or is there something not quite kosher about the paintings?"

"I'll give you the documents on what's already in the basement and what's expected." Marcello avoided a commitment.

"Why not tell Lulu about her father? It would mean more to her than anything."

"That's Penelope's job when the time is right."

"She'll never do it and, if she did, she'd tell it wrong."

"If I knew the right words…" Grandy began, her voice, even her stance, gone soft.

"Tell her anything, mother. Leave out the dark parts. You could begin by treating Penelope more kindly."

"Penelope?" Grandy snapped. "My, my what a lesson you're teaching me. I think I've been quite generous.…"

"I'm not talking about material things. Dear God, have you ever thought how sex and money run this family? She's not a bad person… what you did to her.…"

"Spit it out, Marcello."

"You know that Harry's run off with a black girl. She was pregnant." Marcello paused, as if to weigh whether the balance should be said. "For years Penelope had been crawling into her son's bed…and now that Lulu is an adolescent.…"

"Penelope with her son? How *could* she…!"

"How could *you*? You betray your daughter and then ask her to be custodian of your precious art collection. Don't you think you owe her…?"

"I owe her nothing!"

CHAPTER TWELVE

1954

Marcello seemed to sense the trouble his presence aroused. Simply put, he was too much. Too much beauty and charisma. "He just has to *be*!" one of Penelope's friends declared. But he was expert at defusing other men's envy with quick self-deprecating humor, remembering to include the woman beside him when another approached demanding his attention. When an overly ardent woman hung about his neck after a dance, he'd disentangle her arms and hand her back to her husband with a "Too much woman for me!"

In the house of Penelope and an adolescent girl his hands were full. Another man, sensing the depth of Lulu's anguish, might have turned away, but Lulu's loss of self was a drama written for March, no task but a labor of love.

Twelve isn't a kind age, and for Lulu it was crippling. On the playing field she was an admired champ. Elsewhere she saw her defects, a too-tall, awkward girl in an unbecoming dress picked by Penelope—not out of meanness but for its being on sale. Her refuge became her music room. Here she'd close the door, play the romantic music that now claimed her, and find camaraderie in the paintings Grandy had sent down. Until recently, her favorite had been a pastel of a mother and her little girl, lost in love of one another. But now her focus shifted to another, also dreamy but in this romantic scene a man presses a woman into him in the dance, holding her so that her thighs and lower torso press into his own. Dancing alone, Lulu would hold a pillow just where the couple's bodies met and give herself to the music, arousing a pulse between her legs, a feeling that dismissed her unhappiness over the mirror's reflection.

Just a hint to Marcello confirmed that he, too, identified with the desire to be held, to let go, not a loss but something wonderful gained. He let her see his empathy, just a glance between them when a love song reached climax. "You are my *même chose*," he said to her one day, "my kindred spirit."

"What happened to your father, March?" she asked.

"I never knew him. He was Italian, came from a titled family in Genoa. They were in shipping and owned a famous art collection. He raced cars and was killed in a crash. I've always thought he was Grandy's great love… well, one of them." March smiled. "The way he died, he was driving to the hospital, to be there at my birth. But another car, a drunk driver, they collided. I don't think Grandy ever forgave me."

"You mean that if it weren't for you he'd still…."

"Families. Lulu, you never have to invent anything. It's all in the family."

"Do you and mother have the same father?"

"No. Her father was in the steel business. He was shorter than Grandy, kind of looked like Mickey Rooney. Cute and very wealthy, had an Italian accent. And he loved art, his and Grandy's close tie. Her art collection's enormous, some of it in storage in your basement."

"What happened to him?"

"They said he'd fallen off his horse during a steeplechase, but he was too good a rider. Besides, I heard them talking one night. I was sitting on the stairs listening, yes just like you, Lulubelle. He shot himself out of jealousy, according to the butler, who knew everything."

"I've heard a lot about Grandy's husbands, yes, from sitting on the stairs." Lulu smiled. "Did Grandy betray him?"

"She's always had many admirers. He knew that when he married her but he was crazy about her. You've certainly learned a lot from the movies, Lulubelle."

"I heard mother say to you one day that money was Grandy's aphrodisiac. I looked up the word in the dictionary." "I sometimes wonder if I tell you too much."

"I'd get it out of you anyway, March. You see, I have to know."

But she didn't ask again about her father and never mentioned what she'd overheard on the telephone the day March, Penelope, and Grandy discussed "the nightmare" of her father. Eager as she was to know the secret unspeakables about sex, another part of her wasn't ready. Real life was already too complicated.

A few days later, when they were sitting under a giant oak tree draped in Spanish moss on one of the outer islands to which they had sailed, March said, "I see myself in you, bella."

Lulu sat forward. "You, in me? Oh, but March, you're everything I'm not."

"Time, Lulu. Give yourself time."

"I don't want to be like the women in my family! I have to make myself up, but the people I admire are men. I used to wish I had a penis…don't laugh! Don't even smile because it's serious…."

"I'm smiling out of recognition. I know exactly what you mean."

"Do you? But now I don't want to be a boy at all! I want him to want me. His name's Joe. If only I could call him, be the one who kisses him instead of waiting, waiting…."

"You are just like I was at your age. And the years between us, they aren't that many. As you get older, they'll seem even fewer."

She sat in silence, trying to picture Marcello plain and lonely, as she felt, in spite of all her many friends.

"If I can give you what someone once gave me," he continued, "I'll have repaid the gift. And if I pull it off, I'll be the beneficiary."

"Who was it gave you so much?" she asked.

"A man named Henri Berthault. He was my voice coach when I was growing up at Metro, a terrible father to his own sons but wonderful to me, which often happens. Henri lived life as a feast that goes on and on and taught me to do the same. He was inspirational, but now, *morte*."

"Dead?"

"Yes, gone." Marcello stood, reaching his hand out for her. "We shall sail home like the wind and sing the love songs from all the Broadway shows. Music opens the heart, bella. Never trust a person who doesn't love love songs."

CHAPTER THIRTEEN
1954

In Harry's absence, Lulu had initially hoped her mother would turn and see her. When instead Penelope got caught up in her fascination with the Admiral, Lulu settled for her accustomed invisibility.

She wrote in the diary Marcello had given her: "I must remember what I heard mother and Grandy say on the phone with Marcello. If sex is too scary for them to talk to me about, I don't want to know. All I want is that dreamy feeling when a boy holds me close at dancing school."

No past contest bore any resemblance to selections now made at Madame Dupres' dancing class. At the signal of the piano music, across the room the boys came, all power in their choice, as Lulu stood motionless, waiting for the dear boy Joe. "Please God," she had prayed the night before, "please let him walk to me and hold out his hand." But his course did not run true. She was on the verge of stepping forward when she saw his trajectory, not to her but to Fanny, her best friend standing beside her! Oh, the humiliation, had she put out her hand! Worse was the actuality of having been rejected by Joe in a competition she could not win, no matter how hard she practiced. It was all about her face, her body—everything that hadn't mattered for years. There was no practicing beauty.

She stared at herself in the floor to ceiling mirror, saw herself in a dress that had been on sale and required breasts to fill it out and pretty shoes to anchor it, neither of which Lulu owned. Nor had anyone suggested a trim of her hair which hung lank. Lulu closed her eyes against the mirror image.

"Oh God," she thought, "I'm standing here in this line of girls whose leader I've always been, and I've lost! Lost again!" The lifelong defense against the ball of rage at being left out came tumbling down. She needed Joe to see her as the moon and the stars, the first need of love she'd felt since…but a red light went on inside: Don't go there!

Wasn't she used to being alone? Years ago in the Dark City, when Penelope had picked Harry, the chosen one, and packed the big suitcase with her father's things, and she had kept herself in her mother's sight so as not to be left, they had left her, nonetheless. Penelope and Harry had put on their Sunday clothes and got into the car and, without a backward glance at her, sitting on the front porch with her kittens, right by the railing so they couldn't help but see her, they had driven right by her.

They were back before dark, but by then she had done the evil thing, the ball of rage so hard in her chest she couldn't breathe. The rage was part of herself now. And now the bile had spread to her friends who were her world. "Everybody thinks I'm this nice person, but I am two people, like Dr. Jekyl and Mr. Hyde."

All this Lulu thought lying in bed that night after dancing class, thought it and then buried it. "Dear God, please don't let them see how much I hate them," she wrote in her diary. "No, not hate, because boys are who I love and the girls are my best friends. Please, God, help me!"

But He was of no use when what she wanted was to be held, kissed, she on fire and hungry for the same things her mother wanted.

Locked in the music room, she played her records, heartbreaking ballads that were the romantic background of the Fifties, crooned sighs of dying for love that took her out of her skin, whether weeping alone on the loveseat or dancing by herself, eyes closed in a religious rapture shared with the people in Grandy's paintings.

How she would love to open all the crates in the basement, take the scenes of lovers dancing and lying on riverbanks and cover the walls of her music room with them. She couldn't be left with the picture of what happened at Fanny's party, when the boys drew for partners on the scavenger hunt, and the boy who drew her said, "Oh, no! Somebody trade with me!" Everyone pretended not to hear. Would she go through life with this frozen smile on her face? It hurt smiling that stupid grin when she was angry as hell. All the other girls had fathers and none of them saw what she did back in the Dark City when she was little…. "Oh, shut up, Lulu!" she ordered herself.

She stared up at the metal poles that ran around the room just under the ceiling. Outside the house she'd seen where black discs affixed the poles to the walls "for protection against hurricanes" she'd been told. That's what she needed, Lulu thought, some kind of metal reinforcement to hold her together so she didn't go crazy. The windows in the room were open to the spring night and a woman's scream pierced the night's silence. Lulu was sure it came from The Mansion. That's one place they leave nothing unsaid, she thought; and took Marcello's letter from her pocket, smoothed it, and read it again.

Again and again Marcello tried to tell her what she wanted to believe, and in the end put his assurance on paper: "My darling Lulu, as God is my witness, you are going to be so lovely, so full of life, that you will have your pick of lovers. Maybe not every boy, but you don't want the dullards; what you'll require is a boy to match your lust for life, and they will be yours for the picking. Patience, sweet girl. This is the beginning of your sexual life. Penelope probably wouldn't use the 'sex' word, but I can't have you living in the dark. Because there are so many adventures ahead, it is important that you protect yourself. We'll talk about this more but, believe me, you are going to be a star. Patience. Trust me. Marcello, who loves you."

Every night before bed, she went to her tree house, lit a cigarette, and watched the scene below, alive with electricity. The later it got, the more they laughed, touched, and slipped into the shadows where Lulu imagined their lovemaking, pictures in her mind that often tripped into scenes of Harry and Stella that day at Flossy's for which they would be banished from Charleston, like Adam and Eve from the Garden.

If sex was that awful, why didn't they say it? Was it dirty like money, the other thing no one discussed? Last year a girl had to leave school because she was pregnant. No one said a word to the class, but when a boy got hurt playing with a gun, they told them all about it for hours. What was it about money and sex?

Not wanting to go to sleep with dark thoughts, Lulu imagined Harry with his newborn baby daughter. "Oh, Harry, you'll be a wonderful father!" she murmured. He'd written that he was working in a "hash house, a dump," but that the people who owned it were letting him use their piano. Harry was composing songs for the musical he'd promised to write with her! "It's a kind of blues opera," he'd suggested in his letter, "a natural form, like *Porgy and Bess*. Get Marcello to play the song I've enclosed. And Lu, what do you think about Marcello writing this show with us? He's a musician and I can tell you like him a lot. Keep sending me story ideas and more of those lyrics you'd written as poems.... They fly off the page!"

Fatherhood, more than anything, put Harry in an even more distant world. I'm in no hurry to be a mother, Lulu thought; in fact, there are so many things to do in life and places to go that I may never want to have babies. Then she wondered if Penelope would want to hear about Harry and Stella's baby. Maybe it was best to let Harry tell her. She would write to Grandy who would want to know.

CHAPTER FOURTEEN

1955

"Lulu leads because she is the tallest," said Fanny's mother arranging them in the dance. "And Fanny, you put your hand on Lulu's shoulder and try not to step on her feet."

The two girls stood in each other's arms, serious and patient as soldiers training for war. No one had told them to practice dancing. As naturally as they had once mothered dolls they moved to the seduction of music. Earlier in the south than in the cold climate of the north, and perhaps more passionately, the mating game claimed them.

Fanny's mother watched for only a moment, knowing their desire for privacy in everything these days, and returned to her bridge game as Frank Sinatra began "Secret Love."

"Seems like only yesterday," she sighed.

"It was," one of the women quipped.

Until now it hadn't mattered to Lulu that she was the tallest in her group; there were advantages, as in basketball and tree climbing. Then, when the goddess of adolescence visited each of them as they slept, the most natural thing in the world was for Lulu to lead in the dance as she had in everything so far.

Guided by Lulu's strong lead, Fanny followed her around the living room. Though Fanny was far more lush and reeked of adolescent heat, it was Lulu who insisted they play and replay the romantic songs. Now that she was learning to move to the music she'd always loved, Lulu had cajoled Fanny into practicing the steps they were learning at dancing school. That Joe, the hero of Lulu's fantasies, had chosen Fanny as his partner in dancing class, well, it had to be lived with. Again and again they went through their paces until Fanny's mother called them to the kitchen.

"Grilled cheese sandwiches and tomato soup, Lulu, your favorite!"

After lunch they went upstairs to Fanny's pretty room, so like the bedroom of a young movie star. While Lulu sat at Fanny's dressing table with its pink and white eyelet skirt, silver brush and comb set and three-part mirror, she watched mother and daughter decide which of the new dresses Fanny should wear to dancing school, what pair of patent leather dancing slippers. "Come to think of it," Fanny's mother said, standing behind her daughter, "should we pile your curls on top, thusly, or draw your hair back like this and tie it with this lovely ribbon?"

All three of them cocked their heads and gazed into the mirror, a mother-daughter portrait of two beauties, and Lulu, who quickly moved aside, her pigtails and plainness so sad a comparison she could only take it to Marcello.

"What am I to do?" she asked him, she who had so proudly taken herself out of the silly competition over beauty within her family, a competition suddenly silly no longer.

"Time for a change, dearest girl," March advised, his voice full of promise. He took her to the barbershop in Charleston's finest hotel where, sitting in a high swivel chair beside her, he instructed Mario to comb out her pigtails and to cut a simple pageboy. Then Marcello lit a fine cigar, one of his favorites from Havana, and winked at Lulu in the mirror.

"You have beautiful black hair, like Hiawatha," he said. "See how it falls of its own weight, and so full of lights?"

"But it's straight. All the girls have curls except me."

"Do you really want to be like all the other girls? You're an original, Lulu, unique. We are birds of a feather, you and I."

That did it. She'd rather be like this beautiful man than anyone else. "Are we really alike, I mean, inside?"

"Sweetheart, all the good times are ahead for you and me. Mario, given that our Lulu was endowed with the high forehead of the goddess Minerva, I think that bangs would be perfect."

"Like when the great Garbo played Ninotchka in the movies...yes, yes!" Mario agreed. As the two men beamed upon her image, the heat rose in Lulu's face. The three of them, caught together in the mirror, brought forth a miracle of pleasure, the first Lulu ever felt for the sight of herself.

"I want you to remember this as the beginning of your new life," Marcello said, his arm through hers as they headed south towards Brewster's for a chocolate sundae. "You and I have shared some major moments. One day when we're in Paris or Hong Kong, you'll raise your glass and say, 'You were right. I am beautiful and it began that day in Mario's barber chair.'"

Two days later the dentist removed her braces. Until now she had learned to smile with her upper lip curled over the ugly steel on her teeth, and to kiss in the same fashion so as to protect the boy from the steel as well as to fool him into thinking there was no steel at all. Now, having her hair released from the tight braids and her mouth from the steel cage, kissing became an obsession.

But her faith in Marcello's prediction crumbled. There was nothing about her that fit the image of southern belle. Just the word, belle, connoted those features nature predestined for female excellence in mating, a perfectly formed face as on Elizabeth Taylor, and breasts, big ones as developed on all of her friends, and small feet to go with their small stature, the dainty package that fit perfectly in a boy's arms when they danced on Friday evenings at Madame Dupree's dance class.

Being less beautiful than her friends hadn't mattered when bravery, intelligence, and fleetness of foot counted. Now, utter sameness was wanted. There was no less love among the girls standing at Madame Bertha's waiting to be chosen, but as each was selected by a boy, save for a fat plain girl and Lulu, she could hardly swallow the resentment of the girls she loved, who were her lifeline. But swallow she did, even smile as Joe danced by with Fanny, who was all but weeping for her. Lulu settled for a reject like herself, a boy named Sly Pottinger who lived on the far side of the bridge.

* * *

Sitting in the tree house, the thirteen-year-old Lulu thought, how real Harry's life seemed opposite hers, Harry playing piano at a place called The Black Hawk where guys were called "cats," girls "chicks," and everyone "hip, cool, groovy." In his last letter, he added how he liked to think of her sitting in the tree house singing "Because of You" or "Unforgettable."

"Don't be blue, little sister," he'd written. "You're doing great with my notes on our Blues Opera, picking out the tunes with two fingers. That's all you need for now and the lyrics you sent were really cool. Keep it coming!" Yes, our musical about the mansion where things don't change, where people have arguments and make up.

More than ever she feared the family falling apart, though to be honest, these days she was afraid that it was she who'd lose control. She wasn't used to being a loser. Until boys came along she'd been the most popular girl in Charleston, and forgotten all about the Dark City. "I am not like other girls," she said to the mirror in her bedroom. "I have to be very careful so I don't end up like my father."

Meanwhile, the movies at The Beacon and The Garden were becoming more specific about Good Girl vs. Bad, the latter signaling a coarse and common sexuality with dark lipstick and breasts like long guns on a battleship. Actresses like Gloria Graham and Jane Russell had a low-down and dirty entrance music announcing trouble. At a loss for a model of a female with whom she could identify, Lulu turned to the books Marcello gave her: the heroine Becky Sharpe in *Vanity Fair* might not have been honorable but she had courage and wits. As for the hero in *The Red and the Black*, he suited Lulu just fine as a young person setting out alone to find his fortune.

"See yourself as this boy. It doesn't matter that he's male. Like you, he moves into life as a great adventure," Marcello counseled her one day. "Come with me for a walk, see a movie."

She turned him down, needing to sit near the phone. When it didn't ring and hours passed, her fantasy life took over and she imagined the boy who had last held her holding another girl, injecting her with the same magic he'd used to enslave her. How she hated the boy and the girl, too!

When she hinted to Marcello what went through her mind, he'd said, "Projection."

"Like a movie projector…?"

"In a way. When this guy doesn't call, you project onto him what *you* would be doing in his place. How many times have you told me that if you were a boy you wouldn't settle for any one…."

"Yeah…I probably would cheat. I'd only say that to you. But I can't let go with a boy… I can't end up like Stella and Harry."

She studied for straight A's, all the while praying, "Please, God, please let Joe call," her lips moving silently though the room was empty. And then it happened, not the telephone call but Joe driving by one day. She was closing the wrought iron gate to the house and heard her name, his voice, and turned. The car was idling, Joe's arm on the window ledge, his head turned quizzically to her, one eyebrow up and that half-smile that never became a grin. "Lulu, want a lift?"

"Oh yes," she said and got in the other side.

"Where you going?" he asked.

"Nowhere in particular," she said, which was a lie. She was supposed to see "Marty" with the girls. Now it was up to Joe.

"Let's go see 'Rebel Without a Cause.' How about it?"

"March says it's wonderful."

Finally she was sitting beside Joe in the darkness of a theatre. It wasn't until they were into the story that he took her hand, a doubly moving moment given James Dean was Joe. He talked like Joe, moved like him, and had that same deep sadness and authority. Towards the end, when Lulu began to cry, Joe leaned over and kissed her tears. "It's okay," he whispered into her ear, his lips so close she could feel them form the words. Then the lights went up and they walked out, not even holding hands.

"Lulu," he said when they drove up to her house, "where'd you get that name? It's great. Fits you."

"I don't know. I think my father chose it."

"Where's your dad? They divorced?"

"Oh, Joe, I don't know. I wish I did, at least I think I do."

"You and me, we're not so different."

"But you're so…well, nothing bothers you."

"We'll talk some day. I could trust you, Lulu. You're not like the other girls."

"I'm not?" Her voice was unsure just how to take the words, but he'd said them like it was a good thing. She opened the car door and looked back at him. "You aren't like the other boys either."

"Boy, you can say that again!" Joe laughed. "Be seeing you, Lulu." And he was gone.

She floated into the house, then into the music room where she put on "No Other Love" and began to dance with an imaginary Joe. The dancing couples in the paintings on the wall smiled back at her.

* * *

After supper Fanny came by in her new car and they picked up two other girls, then cruised the familiar streets until they discovered where the boys were hanging out. A blast of the horn alerted the stronger sex to pile into their own cars and the chase began. Most summer evenings this went on until they tired of the chase and settled on someone's house where the parents were absent, meaning they could put on their music and press themselves against one another until the thrill of sexual arousal was once again attained. Joe was not around that evening. That Fanny was in the arms of another boy made Lulu feel less guilty. The new boy was from out of town, visiting for the summer. He was handsome, several years older and soon he and Fanny disappeared upstairs.

Each day Lulu prayed for the telephone to ring and Joe's voice to say her name. It was not that his lips had been the first to rest on hers, his breath the first to leave a taste in her mouth; rather, Joe was a door opening unlike any other. It mattered greatly that he was a bad boy, different from the others, like James Dean. It was uncanny that they had seen the movie together, something meant to be.

Certain thoughts and incidents had become precious and she wrote them down. Marcello had urged her to keep a journal. "The simple act of writing it will flesh it out for you," he'd said. "One day when you're writing in New York, you'll be glad you did this."

"Joe is like my father," she wrote in her special leather-bound book. "…a very bad boy from the way Penelope and Grandy avoid talking about him, meaning it's what they *don't* say. I love Joe. I'm perfect for him, the baddest girl in town, except it's all inside for now. Joe would want me to touch him, would want to take it out and put it inside me, and I can't do that…I just can't! I'd end up like Penelope, like Stella and Harry. There are other things I want to do, travel to New York, Europe and, yes, become a writer!

"Even if Marcello hadn't mapped my future of studies and travel beyond Charleston, I can't stop here, absolutely *cannot* be a wife with babies before I am twenty!

"But I will have my fire," she promised herself in her diary. "Joe's kiss, the way I felt when he touched me, his smell, everything about him makes me hungry for more. I'll wait for him each day and, if he doesn't come, then I'll make do with a lesser boy's kisses, but in my mind it will be Joe's kiss untying the knots inside me. I know now I can unravel in the arms of a boy who knows what he's doing.

"'Coruscating on thin ice'…that's what I'm doing. That's a line in a play by Christopher Frye that I saw at The Little Theatre. Strange how a few words sum up my addiction to being kissed. And with every gift there is danger; in this one, pregnancy, meaning curtains, the end to Eros.

"Ah, Joe, why don't you telephone? Damnable rules that make me wait for his touch, wait for his lips, the softest lips for such a hard boy. Why can't I call *him*? I'd risk rejection, anything to avoid just sitting here. I'm only thirteen, and I'm not allowed to do anything! When I was twelve, the rules were made for breaking; but these new rules make me wait for him to put his arm around me, wait for him to choose me, want me, wait, wait!"

I'd far rather risk rejection than sit frozen, bursting at the seams inside, waiting, waiting for his kiss. Ah, but once kissed, Lulu, she reminded herself, you're inoculated, you can't live without him, can't concentrate on anything else.

It was true. She was unlike all the other girls in her need to be loved, always the last to leave the beach, the car, his arms. Nothing, absolutely nothing measured up to sexual passion now that she'd tasted it.

*   *   *

Lulu was sitting on the best step for hearing conversation in the drawing room below where Penelope was confiding in Marcello. "If only I didn't depend on Grandy for money. It's like a gun at my back."

"What about Charlie's family…they're wealthy."

"They were against Charlie and me marrying. They considered Grandy 'nouveau riche.'" Penelope groaned. "Mother loves having me as her slave. Families…"

"Like countries, 'divide and conquer.'"

"After we married, when Charlie's family disinherited him, he could have cared less. 'You start collecting money,' he said, 'it runs you.'"

"He once told me he had a fine art collection…. It must be worth something…."

"Art? Have you seen those silly paintings in Lulu's 'music room' as she calls it? That's Charlie's 'art.' Well," Penelope snorted, "some of it's Grandy's."

"Lulu likes them."

"Exactly. A child's art. You've no idea of how much Grandy's collected. The basement's full of her crates. She comes to Charleston, before she says hello she's down there making sure no one's stolen any of her precious… God, how I hate my mother's pretense at being 'old money.'"

"Face it, Penelope. You need her. Cut her a little slack…."

"A little slack and she'll steal your most precious…." Penelope was on the verge of tears.

"Remember the grumpy old guy lived down the road," March was saying, "always shaking his fist at us for riding our horses across his property and reported us to Grandy? You took a bucket of horse manure from the stables and put it in his mailbox…"

"Oh, March…!" Penelope laughed through her tears.

"Mother was once a bad girl!" Lulu silently exalted, full of new admiration for Penelope.

*   *   *

The one place Lulu found freedom was The Little Theatre and the only person her age to whom she could talk openly was Sly Pottinger who ran the prop room. Sly was the only person her age who didn't give a damn that he wasn't good-looking. He had, in fact, made something of an anti-beauty statement out of his tall, gawky figure, slicking his hair into oily waves, adding a big pompadour in front like Elvis Presley.

"It's my Teddy Boy look," he said. "You know, British," and he winked at Lulu who was fascinated by the black skinny pants he wore and the gallery of photos he'd created on the wall of the prop room, mostly shots from magazines and newspapers: A girl her age carrying a machine gun in Budapest; a fashion photo of a model wearing a long-skirted "Dior New Look"; many shots of "sex kitten" Bridget Bardot. They were rehearsing "A Midsummer Night's Dream" that summer, and Lulu had won the role of Helena.

"Gee, Sly, you sure have a variety of interests," Lulu quipped and he winked at her, saying something like, "If you only knew." That Sly Pottinger liked her was obvious, but the too-tall gawky lad didn't figure in her dreamsleep, so they became buddies. When the director of the play demanded of Lulu, "More swagger, more self-confidence. Come on, Lulu, you get to play both roles here, male and female! Throw yourself into it!" Sly stood in the wings, down on one knee like a cheerleader.

After rehearsal one night when Lulu and Marcello were at their favorite barbecue drive-in, he said, "You have a gift, sweetheart, real talent as an actor. When you get to New York, see more theatre, you may see it as your future."

"Too much rejection in that world. I want a stage where I stand a fighting chance." She turned to him. "When I come to New York, can I be who I am and find a boy to love me?"

He laughed. "They'll be standing in line. When you go to college, you can spend vacations with me. If a place and a girl were ever matched, it's you and Manhattan."

Sometimes Lulu wondered if even March could love her if he knew about her evil side. "I'm two people," she wrote in her diary, "the person standing on a high wall, smiling, which is who I am with Marcello—and this new angry person who's been inside me all along. I used to be one person. I'm breaking up like..." and she almost wrote "like my father." "Where did that come from?" she asked herself, and dutifully forgot it.

Maybe she was wrong about the life of an actor. She loved the stage, where theatre people were like a family. Maybe she could get used to professional rejection, not the same as with a boy. There was something unique about standing on a stage as someone else, becoming that person and winning all that love in the audience.

"You like risk," she told herself in her diary. "Without it, there are no hidden dragons. Without danger, there's nothing to conquer and, without winning new ground, where are you? Bored," she answered herself.

These thoughts crowded her brain that summer, musings she would take to the stairwell between the second and third floors where she could listen to Penelope and Marcello in the drawing room below. Here were the best acoustics, meaning that when the talk about Joseph McCarthy disclosed that McCarthy was using Marcello "to get at Grandy," Lulu slipped down a step to miss nothing.

"Grandy's sunk a lot of money into fighting McCarthy," March was saying. "If his people can use my homosexuality to get at her...well, she's afraid that sooner or later they'll learn I'm down here. More trouble than you need, Penelope."

"But what can they do to you?"

"I don't want you and Lulu to have to deal with people talking."

"Why, March, people down here don't care about these things."

"They will when McCarthy digs up my connection to Henry Hay. Before, I was just Grandy's homosexual son, a way to get at her in the press. Now they've got wind of my work with Hay on the Mattachine Society. He's been called to testify before the House Un-American Activities Committee."

"Oh, March, I wish you wouldn't use that word...."

"Homosexual?" March laughed. "Would you prefer bisexual? Sure, I love women as well as men, but 'they' say 'you sleep with one man, you're labeled.'"

"I was hoping you'd marry that pretty girl you've been seeing.... You'll break Lulu's heart if you go. And mine, too!"

"We'll see what happens, we'll see...."

"Where did you learn to love love songs?" Marcello asked. "You're the only person, besides myself, who knows all the words to all the heartbreaking ballads, and you're only fourteen!"

They were in his studio at the waterfront, Lulu lying on a sofa watching him paint her portrait which he had so far refused to let her see.

"I don't know, I just love them. They make me feel good, sad but good."

"You're going to like this portrait. It will show you how lovely…"

"Please don't say that! You promised you'd never lie…"

"Remember 'Now Voyager,' Betty Davis is the ugly duckling? Then she leaves home, falls in love and comes back on a ship, walks down the gangplank…. She's beautiful and it's not because of the great shoes and the big hat! She's seen herself in the eyes of someone who loves her…."

"One day I'll go away and come back to Charleston in a big hat…"

"You've always said you felt invisible to Penelope. Do you know how critical it is *not* to be seen for the first years of life, especially when you've a sibling who is doted on?"

"But I love Harry, March…."

"You love him, you hate him. You're part of the human race, Lulu. Don't look so crestfallen. Did you know the first suspect in a murder is someone in the family?"

Fearing the portrait was tied into Marcello's leaving town, she had initially refused to sit for it. Who was this man McCarthy who had so much power he could harm March, and what was the Mattachine Society? So forbidding was his conversation with Penelope that Lulu was afraid to ask questions. She waited for him to explain, but March read her look as the other, equally potent source of her sadness.

"I pride myself on my collection of beautiful ballads," he said, shuffling through a carton of albums sent from New York. "This one is for you." Within seconds the studio was filled with "Out of My Dreams and Into Your Arms." Pulling Lulu to her feet, he circled her in between the sofas, the piano, the easel, Lulu apologizing for her failure to master the art of following in a grand waltz.

"A Viennese waltz isn't easy to master. You should have seen me the first time! You'll love Vienna!"

When he spoke confidently of her future, Lulu's anxiety gave way to anticipation. Vienna! Again she lost herself in the music, remembering the last time a boy had held her in his arms, not Joe, but a good enough boy to arouse the feelings now anticipated. With the right music and lyrics on the car radio, the boy's mouth on hers, his body pressed against her as they lay on the back seat of the car, she could relax the iron control that ruled her. She hadn't known there was any way to be other than the bound-up person she'd been until the music, the dance, and the boy invaded her. When the night was over, she'd return home to find the crotch of her underpants soaked through. That too was magic.

A boy only had to kiss her to become the prince of whom she dreamed day and night. She only had to think about him and she was again besotted, needing desperately another injection for which she would lie, cheat, yes, even betray her best friend. This was a side of romance that wasn't pretty. Strange how passion touched off scary feelings that had always been inside her; how could the romantic songs she loved have anything to do with her dark side, which is how she'd come to name what she sometimes felt towards her best friend Fanny who had won Joe?

Marcello had put on a new stack of records and turned back to his easel. Lulu resumed her pose, head in profile, her gaze focused through the open doors to the sea's horizon. Then something on the wharf caught her eye, three people conversing heatedly at the foot of the gangplank of a ship. Had they looked up, they might have seen her at the wide open doors, but they were involved in their argument. When had Grandy arrived in Charleston? Grandy was coming down more regularly and there was no mistaking it was she, standing erect in her smartly tailored suit, a fox throw around over her shoulders, her auburn hair scooped up in a French twist atop which perched a cocky hat.

"Got to break my pose a minute," Lulu explained to March and grabbed his telescope, focusing on a very angry Grandy shaking her fist at the Bad Admiral who doffed his hat, laughed, and bowed to her. In one movement Grandy took hold of her fox throw, brought it down on the Admiral's head, and raised the other fist menacingly, shouting at him before she strode away, no easy exit in high heels on cobblestones. Once more Grandy turned and hurled what must have been a dire threat, for the Admiral retreated. Only then did he look up and see Lulu who took a quick step back, realizing she was as visible as they. "Wow!" she exclaimed, "What was that all about?" Then the Admiral and the Captain of the ship heatedly discussed something and pointed up to the studio.

"March, you should get a better padlock to this place," she said.

"Assume your position, Lulu," Marsh said, seemingly unperturbed.

When the afternoon was done, he showed her the painting. In the middle distance, a young girl stood in a wisp of a short dress, one foot ahead of the other, mid-step, her hand tentatively raised as if to touch her face, or was it in a gesture of farewell to what was being left behind?

"What's that you wrote at the bottom?" she asked.

"The cusp of adolescence."

She understood what he meant. Everything was changing, new feelings awakening in the middle of the night, during class at school. "I want a life as exciting as Grandy's!" she said to Marcello.

Marcello turned to her. "Don't idealize Grandy, Lulu."

* * *

A few days later, on their way to "A Streetcar Named Desire," Lulu and March ran into Joe and asked him to come along. It was a startling afternoon, not just because she got to sit in the dark theatre between the two men she loved.

"I was convinced the city wouldn't let them show it here," March whispered to her. "How I loved it when it was a play on Broadway."

Then it began and no one spoke until it ended. The three of them sat, mesmerized by the sexual power of Marlon Brando's performance. When the lights went up, Lulu realized she was gripping both men's hands. They stood, still silent, each lost in his own emotional terrain. Walking home, a nod of the head, a knowing smile was all that passed between them. Nor did they stop at the drugstore for the usual Cokes and sundaes.

Only when they reached the corner where they customarily parted did Lulu steal a look at Joe who caught her eye. "That's who you are," she wanted to say to him, meaning Brando. "That's what you do to me." After Joe left, she said to March, "I'll never forget Joe, never. Now I know why."

"He's a very special guy. Does he feel that way about you?" "Oh, no. He's kissed me. I think it's because he knows how I feel about him. I don't mean he pities me, but I know the kind of kisses he's got inside him."

"Passion, sweetheart, sexual passion."

"Yes, that's Joe. Now that I've seen the movie, I know I'm not the only one."

"Other men will arouse you like Joe. But you're right, you won't forget him. Nor should you."

"How come you understand me so well?" Lulu asked, no answer expected.

"Y'know, Lulu, after this movie, they'll never put it back in the box. It's out there, baby, and we're going to see a revolution in this country."

"You mean sex."

"In every shade of the rainbow. You have to give it to Tennessee, he pulled it off like a dream."

"You know Tennessee Williams?"

"The theatre's a small world. You'll meet him when you come to New York. You two will get along just fine."

"It's the kind of writing I want to do some day. Can you think of anything more honest? I mean, can you?"

"You pay a price for sexual honesty. Tennessee's paid his share. But I'll tell you something, sweetheart, it's changing."

"I won't miss it, will I?"

He put his arm around her. "Miss it? You're part of it. Wait till you get to New York, you'll see."

"But March, that woman in the movie, Blanche duBois, was she really crazy, I mean…were they going to put her in a crazy house…?"

"A hospital, someplace safe…Lu, you've got to stop identifying with every…"

"Oh, I wasn't saying I was like her…I just felt sorry for her and scared…"

"Tennessee's drawn to characters like Blanche, people who can't help flying high, love it but…"

"Like Icarus they get burned…" She wanted to add, "And like my father," but the day was too perfect.

* * *

A few days before Lulu returned to school that autumn, the daughter of one of Charleston's oldest families shot herself, leaving a note pledging eternal love for Marcello. Though the bereaved family knew her infatuation for him was unrequited, none of this deterred Marcello from his decision to return north.

"Everyone knows you didn't pursue the girl…" Penelope said.

"Too much for you and Lulu to live with. I can hardly handle it myself…."

"Did you love her? I mean, did she think she had a future with you?"

"Nothing more than a kiss, that's all that passed between us. But I can't have you…and especially Lulu, not at this stage of her life…."

Before leaving, March and Lulu went to the island where they'd had their first picnic.

"I don't want you to confuse the reason for my leaving with the beginning of your own sexual life," he said. They were standing in the shallow water drinking chilled wine. "You and I, Lulu, we can talk about everything…it's always been that way, even when you were a little girl. So, ask me anything."

Lulu stared down into the water. "I thought that men were the people you loved, Marcello…I mean the people you chose to…"

"The people I chose to have sex with. Yes, but I've been in love with women as well, one in particular. You don't have to choose, Lulu, not if you don't want to. Men and women, some of us are attracted to both sexes."

"I'm so glad! Oh, I didn't mean about this poor girl…but I'm glad you sometimes want to dance with…make love to, I mean, be in love with girls, women…."

"One thing you could learn from this tragedy is something no one explained to me when I was your age. I remember my adolescence, the confusion of love and sex. What I know now, didn't then, is that what I was really burning for was an intimate connection with someone. It wasn't sex—otherwise I'd have masturbated—no, what I was dying for was to be deeply connected to someone. That is what you and I have."

She was thrilled.

Marcello packed a few things from his studio, sent them to New York, and gave Lulu the keys to the studio. "There's over a year left on the lease," he said. "I want to think of you sitting in this big arched doorway, looking out to sea and writing lyrics for 'Lost Charleston,' your and Harry's and my Blues Opera."

He took her in his arms, then, without looking back, got astride his Harley. Lulu ran upstairs to the balcony where she'd first seen him, but he was gone and her world with him.

"I love you, Marcello!" she called aloud. "I love you in all the ways you said, in all the ways there are to love!"

* * *

That evening, sitting on the stairs, Lulu listened to the women in the drawing room whispering about Marcello when Penelope momentarily left the room, speaking over one another to grab the choicest parts of the tragedy. They are like vultures, Lulu thought, an image that reminded her of a little man with heavy black rimmed glasses and a black suit much too heavy for Charleston. Yesterday he'd turned up for the second time on a House Tour. Grandy had forbidden Penelope to permit strangers in the house once she'd heard about the tours but, in rare defiance of her mother's orders, Penelope continued to allow them. Yesterday the little man in black had entered Lulu's music room, bowed apologetically and gestured toward the paintings, seeming to ask permission to look. She'd nodded assent. Now the image of him leering at the naked people in the painting returned. Was he spying on Marcello for this evil Henry Hayes?

She had taken Marcello's love to mean he would never leave her. Now she woke in the night, rage and grief warring in the most terrible nightmares, seeded long ago by her mother and brother's exclusive club that rejected her, scenes now larded by eros, not a force to rest easy with a secondary role.

Why had Harry and Marcello abandoned her? Was it something about men, that they walk out on you, for she had to include that first man, father. No, God wouldn't set up the world so that men and women were drawn together like the couples in the paintings, only to betray one another.

There was no one to turn to but Joe. Weren't they matched, he the leader of the pack, she of the girls' playing fields? But Joe had his own rendition of the music that now claimed everyone in their crowd, a rhythm that naturally paired him with the vivacious Fanny, who grew riper with each day, perfect in ratio of nose to lips, shape of eye, length of leg and breasts made for cupping, sucking. Even Lulu was awed by the girl who yesterday had played Sancho Panza to her Don Quixote. One moment Fanny would be circumspect about drawing added attention to herself, and the next she would flirt outrageously with other boys in front of Joe.

Oh, Fanny, don't be so blind to Joe's pain, don't make the other girls envious, or something bad will happen! An image of Fanny punished for hurting Joe took on such preeminence in Lulu's thoughts she was forced to accept her best friend's downfall as her own wishful thinking.

CHAPTER SIXTEEN

Lulu sat at her desk, pages of homework in front of her, though her eye wandered to Harry's letter on the bed. His description of San Francisco played in her imagination, pulling her from Caesar's Gallic Wars. Imagine Harry playing piano at a "joint called The Black Hawk" where Stella sang! a "real dive" he called it. And there was a picture of baby Delilah enclosed.

Caesar didn't stand a chance and Lulu rose and took her cigarettes to the top of the stairs where Penelope could be heard on the phone.

"Oh, I know what you mean, my dear," she was saying. "My husband was like that," and her voice dropped, necessitating Lulu move further down the stairs. "…a supreme cocksman who could build a fire simply by holding your hand! As for the Admiral, well, I have to keep him on a short leash, if you know what I mean…" then some ladylike giggles.

My father a cocksman? Lulu stood and went back to her desk, turning the thought over in her mind as she stared at Caesar in full armor on the cover of her book. She opened it again, a finger of her left hand following the line of Latin as her right hand dutifully penned the translation, work at which she excelled, work that would get her out of this house where she was outclassed in beauty. She was only fourteen but determined to create a different life than her mother's, one on a larger scale, a modern goal running counter to nature, a force she doesn't despise at all and was in constant jeopardy of embracing.

Once again, spurred by the competitive desire to be best among her peers, she pressed forward, cheered on by Grandy and the savings account into which her grandmother deposited economic rewards for excellence.

"Money isn't everything," Grandy had written, "but pay your own way and you can be your own person." When quarterly statements of Lulu's savings account arrived, Penelope said, "Well, well, how's our little banker doing?"

Why weren't the most important things in families discussed? Lulu wondered. Was it some gypsy curse that bad things would happen if families talked about money and sex? Lulu stood, grabbed her pack of cigarettes, opened the bedroom window, and climbed out onto the wall, navigating around the vines and small branches until she arrived at the tree house. She lit a cigarette and surveyed the familiar stage below.

What did Marcello say? "Don't romanticize the people in the mansion." But she just wanted people to call things what they were. When she translated Latin, it was supposed to say in English what the author meant. Well, that's all she asked of her mother, who acted so silly around the Admiral it was embarrassing. No, she didn't want Penelope to tell her about sex. She'd be no better at it than the way she talked about money. You'd think money was dirty and all the while Penelope wished Grandy would give her more.

Lulu surveyed the familiar stage below, the several families in the mansion going about their business as though nothing ever changed. But there were changes, of course, ever since two of the sons had died in Korea. For those boys' funerals, Lulu had gone with the families to the church in Blacktown, then out to the coast near where she and Marcello held their picnics. Standing at the water's edge, Lulu wept and sang with the people who had always included her as one of their own. She had written about the scene, imagining it in their Blues Opera.

Stella had come back for the funeral, had ridden the Greyhound bus all the way from Los Angeles. "I'm not going back to him," she said to Lulu on greeting. "Baby Delilah is staying with him until I get a place." And then Stella walked away.

Lulu hadn't said a word, so shocked was she that Stella had left her baby to…what had she said, "join the movement, the black uprising?"

Wanting to give the families something towards the expenses of the funeral, she had considered selling one of the paintings from Grandy's collection in the basement. Lulu had gone from crate to crate, reading the stenciled lettering, some French, some Italian, but most in English, shipped from Southampton, Marseilles, and Genoa. There were over twenty crates and instead of opening a fresh one, Lulu took a small painting from the crate Grandy had opened when she gave Lulu the paintings for her music room.

"Very precious," Grandy had said at the time, "but it's important you have these two because you are part of the story."

"What story, Grandy?" she'd asked, and Grandy had only smiled, a sad little smile and hugged her.

The old man at the secondhand store hadn't much liked the small painting, but his offer, added to the money from Lulu's own savings, had brought forth enormous gratitude from the families next door.

When Lulu telephoned Harry and described the funeral, she was hoping he'd be homesick, but Harry was full of his own life stories. Nor did he want to talk about Stella leaving him and baby Delilah. "Some voter registration drive in Alabama means more to her than we do." Before Lulu could comment, he added, "Grandy's coming to San Francisco next week, wants to introduce me to some movie people who could give me work. How about that?"

"Can I come, too?" Lulu made a sad little joke to hide the unexpected pang of jealousy that "her" Grandy was getting close to Harry and would probably love her less because of it.

"And I got a gig playing in the pit at the Geary Theatre where—hold on to your seat!—Ethel Merman's opening in 'Annie Get Your Gun!"

"Gosh."

"And Lu…" Harry rushed on, "the movies out here have *live* entertainment between films! Jack Benny was here last week…."

"You saw Jack Benny?"

"Sad thing is, they're tearing down the old movie palaces, putting up dumb little pre-fabs…"

"Just like the Mansion…but we won't let them tear it down, right Harry?"

"Hell no! I tell you, Lulu, having a kid really makes you think about how the world's changing…but back to the Mansion…I've been working on a medley that picks up the old island spirituals, has a counterpart of modern jazz, a kind of meshing that works, sometimes a little discordant…."

"Like when your jazz theme kills the gentler, older…" Lulu offered.

"Now you're cookin'! Hey, the baby's waking up, gotta go! Give my love to mother…I love you, Lu…. Almost forgot, we're moving down to L.A.!"

Lulu hung up the phone, went to the music room, and put on the album of "Porgy and Bess" which he'd sent her. Imagining these beautiful voices being sung in the Mansion reconnected her to Harry, all but washing away the envy of his life's richness.

Even with the occasional screams and loud fights at the Mansion—no *because* of the outbursts—these people's lives felt, well, the only word Lulu could come up with was "natural." They said what they felt without stopping to edit.

When Fanny and she were little, weren't they more 'natural?' They didn't look for other words when they were angry. The older they got, the more screens they put up. Pretty soon there'd be so many screens no one would know who they were. When boys came along, the screens multiplied. Was dancing class 'natural?'… standing there with that stupid smile on her face when no boy chose her? The 'natural' thing for a person was to walk across the room and pick Joe. Didn't she get a silver cup in eighth grade for being a 'leader?' What's a leader to do when she's told to just stand there? She wished the floor would swallow her when it happened. When she felt invisible, she felt scared…no, angry, like…like when she was little and they left her behind, didn't take her to see her father. And so she'd killed the kittens. If Joe loved her, she'd never feel invisible.

Abruptly, Lulu remembered the last time she was alone with a boy, kissing, touching, and, yes, how 'natural' that feeling had been, but the more natural it felt, the more she had to push him away. Her shoulders slumped with a deep sigh. Clearly girls had to lay down the law, say 'no' when they meant 'yes.' "Damn, I was more 'natural' when I was ten!" she said aloud.

"Enough. Got to finish the French translation," she said and left the tree house, returned to her room, sat at her desk and began translating lines of French dialogue.

But there was no controlling these new feelings that didn't respond to her accustomed self-discipline, perhaps because she didn't really want them to go away. The girls in her crowd had stopped talking about private feelings, leaving her once again to wonder if it was the shadow man, daddy, whose influence wooed her away from the books in front of her. Sometimes in her mind's eye she'd imagine him offering her the forbidden fruit, saying, "Take a bite."

Would that someone could explain the turmoil inside her, but please, not her mother, whose reluctant saddling of Lulu into her first "sanitary napkin" had mortified both of them. Penelope's own mother had told her nothing of the kinship between sexual passion and pregnancy, a family tradition Penelope repeated with Lulu. It is all she could do, this woman who tossed and turned alone in her bed at night, to deal with the Admiral, whose proposal of marriage she impatiently awaited.

Again the telephone rang and her breathing stopped. She waited for Penelope to call, "Lulu, it's for you," but there was only silence.

It was a wonder the house didn't explode, given the stages of reproductive heat, two women, mother and daughter, tossing in their narrow beds, ovulating monthly, wired by nature to lie down with the man at hand and, if one wasn't, to ferret out a mate so as to get on with what they were meant to accomplish.

Lulu ordered mind and body away from the memory of the boy in whose arms she recently lay; ironically, nothing would aid her more in her determination to avoid pregnancy than the model of her mother whom she refused to imitate.

Again the telephone rang and Lulu ran to the top of the stairs. But it was for her mother. Lulu turned to go back to work when she heard Penelope say to her best friend, "Oh, why doesn't the Admiral ask me to marry him? I can't believe he already has a wife…that's an envious rumor! As for that other woman trying to steal him from me, well, that little rumor you circulated, it did the trick. You really are a wonderful friend…. I know it's awful to say this, but I hate my mother…she betrayed me once in the worst way. Oh, I can't go into it, but I'm reminded of it every day. Why, I'd marry the Admiral for no other reason than to enrage her. You know…" and Penelope's voice lowered so that Lulu had to go halfway down the stairs, "…the Admiral's onto some 'scandal' my mother's involved in, one he says would put her in jail…I wouldn't tell this to anyone but you…after all, you entrusted me with your own little 'problem'…oh, no, no, I've not told a soul! Wouldn't think of it!"

"Oh, my dear, at least you have a husband while I must depend on Grandy for everything and she ignores my pleas for more. I hate her. As awful as that must sound to you, yes, I hate her with every check from her I cash…. But of course I understand, you being resentful of your husband. So unfair men having all the money…. You know, if Lulu weren't a decent enough child, I'd…I'd…well, I'd do something mean just to hurt my mother who loves her as she's never loved me!"

"Now, you promise. You and I, we never repeat these things to anyone! Bye-bye."

CHAPTER SEVENTEEN

1957

A year ago, a car was just a means of getting from here to there. Then one night, as things happened in adolescence, the automobile was where everything of importance happened. It was a private space commandeered by a masterful boy who could steer with one hand, and with his other arm draw Lulu to him allowing her to rest her head on his shoulder. For a girl as tall as most boys, this opportunity to have what was never enjoyed in childhood promised more than mere transportation.

Because the rules of what one could and could not do with a boy had never been spoken but inferred, as in "Break them and you'll go to hell"— the fear of going too far was a jigger of straight passion beginning with the first touch. So unique was the drug, Lulu would replay the torment in memory again and again.

Caught between childhood and full sexual awakening, Lulu and her friends waited for boys, all life in abeyance until a car cruised by, a horn sounded. On a hot afternoon, should Lulu be alone, she would walk to the playground where they had all grown up and indolently shoot baskets until, sooner or later, a boy, maybe even Joe, would drive by and invite her to cruise with him. This was her favorite fantasy when she was playing Elvis' "Love Me Tender."

One day it happened, and she wasn't even wearing her prettiest shorts; in fact, wasn't dressed at all the way she was in her fantasy. Nor was she alone, a group of girls having found one another and begun a game. Joe stood on the sidelines watching until she dropped out, ostensibly to get water.

"Hey, Joe."

"Let's go for a ride," he said. She hoped he wouldn't ask about Fanny who was off somewhere with a new boy from out of town, a good-looking stranger whose boat was in the annual coastal race. But Joe wasn't the jealous type.

"Want to drive to the beach?" he asked and Lulu replied with a casual, "Sure, fine," lost in the smell of him, the proximity of his bare arm, the blond hairs like delicate shafts of wheat. He wore the sleeves of his white T-shirt rolled up and no socks, his ankles tan as his face. He was talking in his slow way about sailing the Mediterranean, something he, Marcello and she, had sworn they would do some day.

"We'll pick up a few beers at The Pavilion," Joe said when they'd reached the island. It was a weekday and not crowded, probably because everyone was watching the sailboat races. Lulu left her shoes in the car and rolled her shorts higher when Joe's back was turned. Barefoot they were the same height. Joe bought two beers at the empty counter, and they sat on the railing above the beach looking out at the water. He began the conversation they'd had with Marcello, tales of sailing the Mediterranean, the Adriatic, the Caribbean.

Sometime around the second beer, when talk turned to what it would be like to anchor in a busy port like Genoa, Joe took Lulu's hand, walked her to the juke box, and then put both arms around her as they danced to "Secret Love." Lulu buried her nose in his neck, let herself go weightless, floated into him. She couldn't remember the music ending, only Joe leading them out onto the sand, down to the water's edge. They walked towards where the houses ended and there was only tall marsh grass. With every step she could feel his hip move alongside her own and their bare legs brushing against one another. When they were halfway down the coast of Italy in Joe's itinerary, he began to slowly run his hand up and down her bare arm, causing the small hairs to rise. "You cold?" he asked. Lulu shook her head, no longer trusting her voice.

Now the last house was behind them and Joe stopped, turning her towards him. "Lulu," is all he said and stepped into her, occupied her, took her over. He laid her down on the sand, kneeling over her, one leg on either side, blocking the sun. He took off his shirt and, with one arm holding her, slipped the shirt under her head and lay on top of her. His lips were so soft on hers she wondered if it was some practiced art, for she couldn't move and didn't want to.

"I'm going to faint," she said, feeling her bones melt, so often had she dreamed this, prayed for it, never knowing it would feel like this.

Responding to her passion and moving to complete the natural trajectory, he pulled her to him, his swollen penis hard against her own wetness, a kind of heartbeat between her legs never felt before. "Lulu, sweet Lulu," he breathed in her ear, his hand between her legs, moving up her shorts. "God, you're so wet." He pulled down her virginal white pants, unzipping his fly, only to feel her restraining hand.

For the rest of her life she would remember his quick decision not to abandon her but to give her something to remember him by, though little did he know how fruitfully it would be used for the rest of her life. "Okay, okay, baby, I won't come inside you," he whispered, "but let me give you this." He moved down between her legs and put his lips, his tongue, and his considerable talent into her first experience of oral sex, a flight of such height and duration she would use it as her orgasmic map for the rest of her life.

When she opened her eyes, he was lying on the sand beside her, propped on his elbow, smiling, shaking his head in disbelief, his fingers gently circling her juices round and round that area that so many girls can't bring themselves to admire. "Some day we'll complete this," he said.

"I love you, Joe. I've always loved you," she said solemnly, staring up into his green-grey eyes.

"I know. We're just out of sync right now."

They parted that day in a silence packed with understanding so deep that she would never feel separate from him, even when she lay in another boy's arms in the backseat of Joe's car, hearing the sounds of his lovemaking with her best friend Fanny.

* * *

That night, her adventure with Joe, coupled with the noise of Penelope's late night party downstairs, kept Lulu awake. Eventually she went to her listening post at the curve of the stair. The evening was ending, a door slam exiting the last partygoer.

"Alone at last," Penelope cooed to the Admiral, and made a giggly noise that wrinkled Lulu's nose. She was tired and about to leave her post and go to bed when the Admiral said, "One last drink, Penny, my darling," and then, "you're such a woman of mystery. You've never told me about your family. Come, let's sit and begin the story of the woman I love."

"Oh, Horace, it's such a sad tale. I don't want…"

Now Lulu was on the Admiral's side. "Make her talk, make her tell it so I can hear too!" and she slipped down two more steps.

"You know, Horace, all I've ever wanted is to *not* be like my mother. I've dedicated my life to it. When I was little, Grandy scared me. I think it's because she never looked at me. I felt so invisible, I was afraid that one day she'd trip over me, not noticing."

"My poor darling, keep talking…"

"Everybody loved her, at least gravitated towards her. How could they not? She was Auntie Mame, always the center of attention." Penelope sighed. "She should never have had children. But women are expected to become mothers, even women like Grandy who cared more for her horses than her children…horses, money, and art."

The Admiral was making little sympathetic noises like, "Oh, my poor darling…poor little Penny. And your father?"

"I've only the vaguest memories of him," Penelope continued. "He was badly injured in World War I…bedridden until he died. I don't think his absence phased mother. He left her a huge amount of money, her aphrodisiac, which no doubt eased the pain of loss…and with the money she began her art collection."

"Ah, her obsession with art and the paintings in your basement…."

But Penelope was lost in the sequence of family events. "I vaguely remember Marcello's father, her third or fourth husband. He was a sweet man and also very wealthy." Penelope paused. "As I said, Horace, my goal in life is to *not* be like my mother."

"Well spoken, my darling, and for it—for I know it was not easy to tell—may I kiss your cheek and this, and this…?" which is when Lulu wanted to put her finger down her throat; went back to bed, committing to memory the stories just heard.

CHAPTER EIGHTEEN

1958

Fanny lay on the bed, sobbing. Lulu sat beside her and tentatively stroked her soft, blond curls.

"There, there," Lulu crooned in a voice until now used only for small animals. "Shhh, everything will be all right. What happened, Fanny? Can I help? I'll do anything. It can't be that bad."

"Oh, but it is, it's the most awful thing, I hate him, but a baby needs a father! But he's a big baby himself." She said this last angrily, sitting up.

"You're pregnant?" So grave was the news that Lulu couldn't pretend composure. For Fanny's sake, she forced herself to be calm, though her hands were cold as ice.

"Help me! Oh, please, somebody help me!" Abruptly calm, Fanny said, "I'll get an abortion. I know someone who had one. I'll call her."

"I'll come with you."

"You will? Where will I get the money? I don't dare ask mother…she'd want to know who the guy was…she'd blame Joe…."

"You mean it's not Joe?" Lulu was taken aback. "Oh, God, now I get it!" Lulu's thoughts tripped back to the several times she'd seen Fanny in his car. "The Bad Admiral," Lulu said calmly, as in worst fears realized.

"How did you know? Don't answer. I wasn't exactly subtle, was I?" Fanny said with resignation. "I don't even like him."

"But why, Fanny…why *him*?"

"I've thought about it a thousand times. Why would I give into him and not Joe or some other boy I loved?" Fanny looked down at her nails that were uncharacteristically bitten down raw. "Know what? I think I picked up a dirty old man because that's the way my mother talks about sex…no, not talks but doesn't say anything to me about it, just grinds her teeth and looks away like, like…."

"Like it's filthy, or they'd tell us, wouldn't they…but I don't believe it's dirty…. Oh, dearest Fanny, I'm so sorry, I could cry…"

"You don't know what a mean, self-satisfied man he is, and cruel. Why, the things he says about your mother…."

"I'll kill him. I really will," Lulu said evenly, each word leaded with fierce determination. "But first we have to take care of you. All that money Grandy has sent me for years, I've got it all."

"I've got money…"

"If it's not enough, I'll steal it."

"Oh, Lulu, you really are something!" Fanny's arms were around her neck, her mascara on Lulu's cheek. "I'll never forget this. I'll pay you back. I swear I will."

It felt so good, Lulu blushed. "Don't worry about that. First of all, how do we find this doctor? Call your friend, get his name and a telephone number."

Before nightfall a date had been made ten days ahead for Fanny and Lulu to drive to a small town, Fayetteville, twenty miles north. Several times Lulu was on the verge of calling Marcello but resisted, respecting Fanny's wish to keep everything between them. What luck she'd got her driver's license on her fourteenth birthday.

Meanwhile Lulu went to the library to read up on abortions but found the description too upsetting to continue. "Please, God, don't let this happen to me," she prayed walking home, people staring as she passed, her lips moving.

Lulu might toss in her bed at night in the same heat as Fanny; they might share the same dreams of seduction, but no matter how passionate the dreams, Lulu would not let herself succumb to intercourse. She would burn before she gave into what she desired most. Sympathy for Fanny had strengthened that determination.

Lulu would have liked to talk to Fanny about the silence among their friends who used to tell each other everything. Outwardly it would have seemed they were the same tight group who hung on the telephone. But there was a new reticence among them, no mention of the passion each girl felt set her apart, a hunger for more than was allowed, a giving up of the self.

In these last days before the abortion, Lulu retreated to her old haunts down by the waterfront where she could watch the ships unloading cargo. One day, the Bad Admiral turned up again, almost unrecognizable in civilian clothes and dark glasses. He was arguing heatedly with the freighter Captain whom Grandy knew, the Captain shaking his head, a defiant "No!" and the Admiral poking the Captain in the stomach with a threatening forefinger. Lulu's hatred of the Admiral had doubled since Penelope scolded her for spending so much time on the wharves: "The Admiral says quite rightly that it's dangerous for a young girl to be skulking around those ships."

"Did he tell you what he was doing there?" Lulu asked. "He belongs out at the Navy Yard, not with the merchant ships. Unless, of course, he's into illegal drugs."

That night she telephoned Grandy. Something told her that her grandmother would want to know the two men had met without her. "You were right to call," Grandy said. "I've cargo arriving from Europe. That Admiral had better stay out of my business or…" but she caught herself and in that moment Lulu decided to tell her about selling one of the paintings to the junk man.

There was a pause. "You…sold…my…painting?" Each of Grandy's words was like a bullet, and Lulu waited speechless. Now the anger built. "How dare you, you ungrateful child!" and then another pause before a barely controlled voice returned. "Those paintings are not your property. If you ever part with one of them…no, no, let me see," and she paused again, thinking out loud, "I could move them, bring them north…."

"Dear Grandy," Lulu tried to make amends. "I will guard them. I'll never let anyone touch them again, now that I know how precious they are."

Grandy sounded very tired. "Yes, yes, you do that," and she hung up.

* * *

When Harry called a few days later, Lulu was still stinging from Grandy's reprimand. Now Harry's enthusiasm about Grandy's generosity to him and his daughter didn't sit well. Envy of Harry on top of her own guilt was a nasty mix, and Lulu was about to hang up when Harry said, "Controlling one's life requires paying one's own way…" those were Grandy's very words and then she said, 'Money isn't everything but it's essential to independence. Lulu is like me.'"

"Do I really want to be like Grandy?" Lulu wondered for the first time. Then she listened as Harry segued to their blues opera. In her last letter Lulu had written him about the old buildings in Charleston that were being "restored," though some looked more like they'd been demolished. "The families in the Mansion are afraid their home is on the list and they'll be moved out. It's awful to think of the Mansion being destroyed…"

"But what a great climax for our musical!" said Harry. "It's happening everywhere. Some of the beautiful old movie palaces here are being turned into lots of little pre-fab boxes…" He paused. "Hey, let's talk about the good stuff. I'm sending you a medley I wrote…old island spirituals with a counterpart of modern jazz, a meshing…sometimes works, sometimes goes discordant, the modern theme killing the gentler, older…. Get it? Whoops! Little Delilah's climbed on to my lap and sends a kiss…. Oh, and Lu, looks like the L.A. move is on. Grandy's found us a house in Little Venice…."

"Oh, enough about Grandy!" Lulu said dismissively. "It's easy for her to play the benevolent…. Why don't you ask her where she gets her money?"

Harry paused. "Listen, Lu, you better get that anger of yours under control, figure out who you are, Queen of the Jungle or Poor Little Match Girl. Anyway, I love you, gotta go."

Full of shame, Lulu put the receiver back. Where does my anger come from? I'm not like other girls. Sometimes I barely control what's waiting inside, ready to change me into a demon from hell, like in the movies when crazy people get put in straightjackets before they kill. My best friend gets the best boy, and I'd betray her on a dime, turn from bosom buddy into.... All this anger, my sword of retribution, the necessity to get even at any cost, is this my father's? She stood and walked away from the tainted phone. "Why can't I swallow my anger before it erupts? I think I'm over it, that the blackness was kid's stuff, then up it comes again, so sudden I could kill...not really, not you, Harry! My poor father, I'd be angry too if they put me in a crazy house."

Though she had promised the car to Lulu a week in advance, on the day of the scheduled abortion Penelope decided to take The Bad Admiral to lunch at the beach. "I'm sure one of your friends can drive you wherever you're headed. The Admiral and I may be late, but supper will be served on time," she said, leaving Lulu no alternative but to call Sly Pottinger, the only trustworthy person she knew who owned a car.

"He'd never tell a soul," she promised Fanny. "Besides, it's a good idea to have someone with us, just in case, well, you know, in case I have to look after you." Lulu didn't want to tell Fanny any of the misadventures she'd read about in her research.

Sly lived on one of the outer islands, and had become part of their group at dancing school where he stood out like a scarecrow. Since he was taller than Lulu, they had inevitably been partnered and had stepped on one another's feet so often that it had become a joke between them. That someone could care so little about social acceptance impressed Lulu, along with Sly's inordinate amount of information about the two whorehouses in Charleston. For years Lulu and her group had cruised by the "houses of ill repute," squealing with horror and excitement at what they imagined going on behind closed doors. Sly, on the other hand, had often been inside and knew the girls' names. "I keep them in grass," he said, "marijuana to you."

When Lulu asked if he would help her take Fanny to the doctor, first swearing him to never tell a soul, Sly readily agreed. "Sure, I'll help. I've had friends in this situation before. I even know where the doctor lives. Don't worry, Lu, we'll take good care of Fanny."

When Saturday arrived, true to his word Sly was early, waiting outside the house in his car. "I've brought extra cash," he said. "Just in case," and then to Fanny he said, "Don't you worry, this guy's got a good reputation. Lulu and I'll take care of you."

They arrived early at the doctor's office in a village outside of Charleston. When the nurse beckoned them in, the doctor ordered Lulu and Sly to remain in the car at the foot of the drive. He did, however, ask for payment in advance, which Lulu gave him.

They waited, staring at the doctor's door, until Sly asked Lulu if she was a virgin. At her shocked "Yes!" he asked, "What else should we talk about, given what's going on inside the house?" He talked readily about his own sexual experience, amazing Lulu who had always thought Sly's looks worked against him.

"I deliberately choose to look like this," he said. "Besides, the girls I go after aren't drawn to me by my swell clothes. It's my cock. It's enormous."

When Lulu burst out laughing he started to unzip his fly. "No!" she yelled.

"But you really should have a look, Lu."

She acquiesced but looked away until Sly said, "Okay, girlie, eat your heart out."

"Oh, my lord!" she gasped. "You can't possibly put that inside a girl! It would kill her!"

"Wanna touch it?"

"Oh, Sly, put it back where it lives," she giggled.

"You'll be sorry."

At the height of their hilarity, the nurse appeared outside the door and beckoned them.

"Well, at least it made the time pass," Sly said, seeing the chagrin on Lulu's face at being caught so full of mirth. They got out of the car, and followed the nurse inside. Just the smell of the place was enough to restore terror. Fanny was chalk white, her eyes swimming in tears and drugs, and

Lulu and Sly quickly focused on getting her down the drive and onto the back seat of the car.

"Give her one of these in another hour," said the nurse handing a packet of pills to Sly. "After that, one every three hours. She'll be all right."

Lulu wasn't at all sure of the last comment. Fanny was in terrible pain, lying in Lulu's arms, bleeding copiously. "Fanny, I think we should take you to my house," Lulu said.

"No, no, not there, not with Penelope," Fanny gasped. "He might be there."

"I've got just the place," Sly said. "I've seen women there in Fanny's condition and they've got a doctor who'll come to the house."

In twenty minutes they were there. "Oh, no, Sly, what are you thinking? We can't take Fanny in there! It's a...."

"A whorehouse. I know you'd rather be at the hospital, but you don't have a choice. They're real nice women. Trust me." He disappeared into the house, then quickly returned.

Beyond caring where they were taking her, Fanny was supported between Lulu and Sly up the drive and into the House of Ill Repute. "She gave me a lot of lip, you know, about the police and 'What if the girl dies?'" said Sly, referring to the Madame. "But I gave her six ounces of my very best grass."

Once inside, a pretty young girl in a wrap dress led them into a back bedroom. "No one will see you back here. Oh, my poor darling, here, let me help," she said and, with Lulu on one side and herself on the other, they managed to settle Fanny on to the bed and slip off her dress.

"My God," said Lulu, "look at all that blood! We need a doctor!"

"We've already called. He's on his way. You're Lulu, right honey? My name's Beth Anna and, well, this doctor has handled cases like this before and he's good. I wouldn't tell you if it weren't so."

Finally he arrived, a gray-haired man with a black bag. "Everyone leaves the room, except you Beth Anna," he said sternly, and Sly took Lulu's hand, led her out, and closed the door.

"If anything happens to Fanny..." Lulu began.

"Nothing bad's going to happen. I promise," Sly said. "This guy's on staff at the hospital. Besides, he has that unlikely organ for a doc, a big heart. We'll pay him, but he doesn't do it for the money. His sister died in a botched abortion. He's really at risk being here." Lulu followed him towards the sitting room up front. "Know what the girls here say about him? 'If his penis was as big as his heart, he'd be the most popular guy in town.'"

Lulu managed a smile and sat on a red velvet sofa beside Sly who was rolling a joint from his pouch. "Not now," she whispered, aghast at what he was doing. "Not here!"

"What better place than a whorehouse?" he said matter-of-factly. Even as he spoke, several girls meandered in and draped themselves on either side of him. "Look, Lulu, I know this is a bad time for you but this will take the edge off. Trust me."

This would be Lulu's second experience with marijuana, her virgin smoke having been at Sly's insistence months earlier at dancing school when his awkward efforts at learning to waltz had led to a brief retreat out onto the verandah. The rest of the evening the two of them floated around the floor, much to Madame's approval.

The grass proved an instant relaxant. When Sly asked how Fanny's assignation with The Bad Admiral had come about, Lulu repeated what Fanny had told her. The Admiral had turned up at the Yacht Club one day, and finding Fanny alone had responded to her usual flirtation. A drive to the island was offered where drinks at one of the oceanfront bars had led to a longer drive to an even more secluded spot. Encouraged by Fanny's passion in the front seat, he had taken a blanket from the trunk of his car, spread it beneath the palm trees and, "fresh out of condoms," had promised he wouldn't come inside her.

"Guess what?" asked Lulu.

"It figures. God, you'd think a girl like Fanny would know better than to trust in a quick withdrawal."

"A girl like Fanny? She was a virgin, Sly."

"Holy shit! You could have fooled me." Sly sighed. "Poor Fanny. Underneath all that Miss Superiority stuff…"

"She's innocent."

The high from the grass now turned downwards, and they sat staring into space. Within minutes two of the girls came out and sat, one on each of Sly's knees. Try as she might to rise to their light-hearted level, Lulu couldn't get Fanny out of her mind. She stood and walked to another doorway where she peeked through to an even larger room where four or five men sat reading magazines, drinking, smoking, chatting among themselves and with the girls.

She had expected the men to be sitting nervously staring at the floor or wearing dark glasses and hats to hide their identity. But there was no attempt at anonymity. The men were in fact more relaxed than at one of her mother's cocktail parties. Why didn't women have a place like this where they could give up all that nervous rigidity? Lulu wondered.

Then she saw him, The Bad Admiral, Penelope's Admiral and now Fanny's too, the leader of the fleet and contender for her mother's hand in marriage. He was in civilian clothes, but there was no mistaking what Penelope called "his noble head."

Lulu's instinct was to put her strong hands around his neck, bang his head against the wall, and kill him, an impulse that had been there for a long time. She stood shifting her weight from foot to foot, a boxer dying to get out of his corner and kill the bastard, but Sly grabbed both of her arms from behind.

"Fucking asshole," Sly said in her ear. "I was hoping His Eminence wouldn't be here today. The word is he's leaving soon, going back up north where I hear he's got a wife."

Lulu turned to Sly and grabbed both his arms. "He's got a *wife*, and been here all this time just playing around with Fanny and my mother?" Waves of feeling swam in, grief for her mother and a killer revenge. "But why would he be here?" Lulu asked. "This is a place with, well, prostitutes. Why come to a place where you pay money?"

"Paying for it makes it nice and tidy, a business deal as in the lady ain't going to call your wife and rat on you."

"But then he comes and visits my mother and brings his vile, nasty germs into our house…."

She could see Sly was offended, as if she had criticized him personally.

"These girls are checked by doctors once a week and you'd be surprised how 'nice' most of them are. Listen, kiddo, I bet half the fathers of your friends come here, one time or another."

"He's already got a wife, and my mother thinks he's going to marry her!"

Before Sly could answer, Lulu stepped into the room. The Bad Admiral shot to his feet, moved across the room and instinctively, as in steering a ship, maneuvered her into a corner.

"What are you doing here, young lady?" he tried for command. "Good thing I happened to be, uh, escorting two of my errant sailors back to the ship...."

"Fuck off," Lulu countered, stalking him back into the center of the room where the other men were watching the show. "Fanny was a virgin," she snarled. "My mother believed in you, you deceitful bag of shit."

"This is the trouble with your generation," the Admiral parried, but the thrust was off the mark and the bemused expressions of the other men were further unsettling him.

Unaware that she'd already won, Lulu spat her final words: "You're old enough to know when a girl is lying about her expertise! If I hear of you telling anyone about this, my mother in particular, I'll report you to the Navy for forcing yourself on a minor! Rape would look good on your record, you...you scumbag!"

"Wow! I'm bowled over by admiration!" said Sly quietly after the Admiral made his exit. "Where the hell did you get those lines?"

"'From Here To Eternity,' 'The Blackboard Jungle,'" Lulu answered, flushed with accomplishment. "You know, Sly, you see things in the movies and one day when you need ammo, Pow!, out they come!" She began to laugh so hard she had to be helped into a chair by the women who now surrounded her, patting her on the back.

"He's a cheapskate!" they chorused. "And he doesn't bathe!"

Everyone was in such good spirits, the note of hilarity so high, that doors opened and more women came running out asking, "What happened? Who's getting married?" When they heard about the Bad Admiral a general hurrah went up and Sly sat down at the piano, playing "Happy Times Are Here Again."

The emotional weight of the whole day was beginning to unwind when someone Lulu hadn't seen before, a graceful woman who looked like one of her mother's friends, came up to her.

"May I?" she asked. When Lulu nodded, she sat on the arm of her chair. "My name's Josie," she said, taking Lulu's hand. "Short for Josephine. What say we go into the next room where it's quieter?"

They sat on the sofa. Still holding Lulu's hand, Josie said, "First, the doctor says your friend will be fine. She's asleep right now and should stay here until maybe eight or nine o'clock."

"When can I take her home?" Lulu asked, worried anew that Penelope would ask questions.

"After the doctor has come back and looked at her. He asked me to reassure you. He just wants to check before she goes home."

Lulu squeezed Josie's hand. A wave of exhaustion had come over her, her eyelids heavy from the grass and the emotion.

"Poor kid, you're really spent, aren't you? Would you like to nap here, or should I ask Sly to take you home?"

"No, please don't go. I like being with you. Your accent, you're from away, aren't you?"

"New York. I came here to visit, fell in love with the place, and never looked back. Charleston is, well, lost in time, a fairytale place."

"I feel like I've known you a long time. Do people tell you that a lot?" She yawned. "Thank you for taking care of my friend."

Josie smiled. From another room came the sound of a piano and the score from "Damn Yankees."

Still holding Josie's hand, Lulu leaned against her and put her head on Josie's shoulder. "You're going to wake up tomorrow morning," Lulu heard Josie's lovely voice, "and wonder about this whole business, Fanny's misadventure, being here. All I can tell you is, don't let this put you off romance, love of which is written all over you. Men are good currency, no worse and no better than women."

"I've never met anyone like you," Lulu said sleepily. "Are you sure you're not some fairy godmother sent to look after me?" She looked up through half-lidded eyes. "Wow, what a day! How'd you get here, Josie? Not just to this house, but to Charleston?"

"I came down to meet my fiancée who was disembarking from his tour of duty. But he didn't come back and they hadn't had time to notify me. He'd been killed by a landmine just hours after the surrender."

"Oh, I'm so sorry. I didn't mean to pry."

"Don't apologize. I had found Charleston and, like you, I love this place."

"Excuse my asking, but you could have found a job anywhere, I mean, oh, Lord, there I go, putting my nose in other people's…"

"You wanted to know why I didn't take a job in some nice office, instead of here? The answer is, I was pregnant with my fiancée's child. When he wasn't on that ship, the shock of learning…I had a miscarriage. The doctor who took care of me, he's the same doctor you met here, gave me a job in his office. One day, one of the women from here came to see him, and she and I became friends. When I heard what good money she made and that it was the nicest house in town, well, I enjoyed sex, liked men, and here I am!"

"Can I ask more questions? Do you mind?"

"Ask away."

"You're so well educated, more than the others, and they're all so young…."

"Young, old, fat, thin, you'd be amazed at what men want in a woman sexually. Not something they'd ask of their wives, but the kind of sex that, that well, fleshes out their fantasies."

"Fantasies? You mean dreams?"

"Dreams but things they like to imagine during sex. How old are you?"

"Sixteen."

"Don't you have daydreams about how you want to feel with a boy, how he made you feel when he kissed you?"

"Oh yes, I've had those dreams even before a boy kissed me. I remember sitting on the big round arm of the sofa at home when I was four years old, straddling it and rocking back and forth, getting this nice feeling down there and imaging pirates...."

"Exactly! Well, men who come here, they have fantasies they like to tell the girls."

Lulu was fascinated. "During sex you mean! I've never told anyone mine, but sure, I can see how coming here, where no one will tell your wife and you can do private things..." Lulu began to laugh knowingly and so did Josie.

Sly appeared at the door, setting them off into further peals of laughter.

"Wow, I've never had that reaction entering a room," said Sly. "You two get along like the proverbial barrel of monkeys."

"Sly, I'm having the most wonderful conversation with Josie!" Lulu shrieked.

"So I see. The other girls want me to play the score from 'Oklahoma.' It's Lulu's favorite, and I thought she'd like to lead the chorus. But I don't want..."

"No, no, let's sing," Josie said. They stood and followed Sly to the main room where he sat at the piano, the women clustered around him. Somewhere in the middle of "I Can't Say No" Lulu whispered in Josie's ear, "The men who come here, do they all want the prettiest girl?"

"Not at all. We each have what you might call 'our specialty.'"

"Like flavor of the week?"

"Precisely."

"And they don't all want the same thing?"

"To be blunt, they all want to reach orgasm and to get there each man has his own fantasy like we were discussing."

"Where do they come from...the fantasies?"

"Well, I never thought...but some come from early years, adolescence, even childhood, when sexual feelings start and we already know that part of our body is 'bad' so it's exciting to break the rules...."

"If it's so important, I mean...if it starts so early, why do adults say, 'Oh, it's just sex...' like it's a bad cough?"

"I guess because 'their' parents never discussed sex with them..."

"But Josie…are there places like this for girls, where men do for us what you do? I mean, so much more is forbidden to girls than boys…."

"Hey, that's a good question. Don't be embarrassed, honey. Lord knows, there are women as horny as men who'd enjoy a place where they could be sexually satisfied, privately, no strings attached."

"Even 'nice women?'"

"Sex has nothing to do with niceness. It would be a happier world if women took the edge off now and then. Most men enjoy giving a woman pleasure. Don't believe that line about men being beasts for wanting 'it.' Leave a woman alone with a man in a private place where other women can't judge her, you'll see a tiger who never wants to leave the jungle."

"There's an old house near us," Lulu began, "a mansion where several black families live. They're wonderful people, Josie, so relaxed and, well, physical, kind of like this place…but I don't mean men pay, it's more in the way they talk and touch each other. At night, when I'm in my tree house, well, the sounds…laughter and people crying out like they're gonna die…I know it's sex…but it's a part of how they live, it's all bound up together."

"You make it sound like heaven." Josie smiled.

"I just love being with those families, being close to that feeling…."

Josie took Lulu's hand. "This feeling you talk about, people touching, caring about one another, lying down together at night…maybe once upon a time it was natural but long ago we lost it…."

"I think if women had a place like this to go to," Lulu said, "we'd be a lot more relaxed."

"You are the funniest kid," Josie roared with laughter, then added, "and you're very smart. Oh yes, very smart."

Sly approached. "Sorry to interrupt, but our princess upstairs is ready to go," he said. "She's pretty sedated but the doc says she'll be okay. You two having quite a talk."

"Maybe the best talk I've ever had," said Lulu and hugged Josie. Then the three of them settled Fanny in the car.

"I'll tell you something I do regret. It's not having a girl like you," Josie said to Lulu. "Take care of yourself."

"I'll come back and see you. Maybe talk some more about The Mansion?"

"Absolutely. Maybe we can get Sly to arrange a picnic for the three of us."

Lulu sat in the backseat with Fanny's head in her lap. "How do I let mother know The Bad Admiral has a wife?" Lulu asked Sly. "God, I hate him."

"We'll find a way to clue your mother in to the bastard," Sly said. He gave her a thumbs-up. "The Bad Admiral's met his match."

"I really liked Josie. She has a certain authority…"

"She runs the place, well, like a den mother, keeps the women in line and the men. She's a nice woman but, boy, can she be tough."

Lulu closed her eyes the rest of the way home, Fanny's hand clasped tightly in her own. "I'm not going to have to get an abortion," she swore silently, nor would she have to get married because she was pregnant. Harry and Stella, Fanny, and she'd bet Penelope too…. She looked down at Fanny, asleep in her lap. Oh, she'd much rather be the one in charge than stand with her hand out like a supplicant, like Penelope, and yes, like poor Fanny. Money wasn't everything, as they kept telling her, like she was a bad person for saving it. But she vowed to herself: "I won't be like the women in my family, I won't, I won't."

CHAPTER TWENTY

1959

The year before graduation, Lulu burned the midnight oil. Her school's headmistress had assured her that if she kept up her very good grades, along with her role as a leader, she might get into Radcliffe. "They are especially eager for more southern young women," she'd said. "If you lived up north, you would have a hard time getting in. But they are looking for more southern girls. And you've an excellent, well-rounded record, being Head of Student Government, a fine athlete, an actress and, yes, top of your class. But if you are accepted, Lulu, you're going to have to work as never before." When the acceptance arrived, Lulu telephoned Marcello who'd been urging her to aim for a fine northern college.

He was thrilled for her. "There's more, Lulu, so much more," he said. "Family is a great choice, but first, first find out who you are. 'Now, voyager, now.'"

He was pleased she'd picked Radcliffe, not just for its standing, "But Boston is a cosmopolitan city, great museums, a favorite site for Broadway shows to try out, and need I mention all the men's colleges in the environs? Best of all for me, you'll only be a few hours' train ride from New York."

March had enclosed a clipping from a New York paper, a photo of him at the Plaza Hotel's Persian Room, along with a quote, "Catch his act, and you'll understand why Judy Garland picked him as her lead back-up singer. The guy's got a gorgeous voice." In the letter, March seconded her decision to fly to the West Coast to see Harry before college. Part of Grandy's graduation present was a ticket to Los Angeles, and then to Boston.

Before leaving Charleston, Lulu and Josie met several times. "I've been offered a job at Hugh Hefner's in Chicago," Josie confided. "I'll be a kind of 'House Mother' to the Playmates."

"Take notes, Josie! If I'm going to write a blues opera about The Mansion next door, I've got to know more about sex."

Lulu had set a typewriter atop her mother's folding bridge table in her music room. Before she forgot the details, she wanted to write about the house where they'd taken Fanny. She couldn't get out of her mind how at ease the men were.

"This business of making yourself be honest when you write is scary, but rewarding too, as in…as in knowing the Dorian Grey part of yourself. I must start with what I know best: family and…and what families most often *don't* talk about: sex and money. They're both dirty, hence the silence, hence they must be very important indeed. The people at the Mansion desperately need money so that the developers don't take their home. Life certainly is confusing." On this note, Lulu went to bed.

Halfway down the stairs the next morning, what she'd written came back and she hurried to the music room, half-suspecting it wouldn't be there. There it was in the typewriter, all but waving at her, "Over here, over here, you hussy!" She began to read, guilt labeling her in the first lines but quick upon it a thrill at having said it and broken the Nice Girl rules!

All day long she kept the doors in her mind open, a part of her brain waiting for the straggler thoughts, always the best and the last to catch up. Finally they came, half-shame-faced for showing themselves: thoughts from the Dark City.

Lulu began to type: "I arrived in this beautiful town a four-year-old child, but what I brought with me from the north is what made me different from the other girls. March says, "Four years has memories, and you shouldn't hate being different. Being 'original,' is a good thing. Everybody has a Dark Side," he said. But I'm not so sure. Everyone else has a father. My Dark Side is all about my father. Maybe it's because he's been kept a secret. I won't know for sure until I find him. And I will find him! Until then, writing helps."

* * *

In the months before flying to Los Angeles, Lulu would be maid of honor at four weddings. Three of the brides were pregnant, though the story of their union was told as the consummate romance of young sweethearts. The first of these was Fanny and Joe's.

Though Lulu had never confided in her best friend, not wanting even Fanny to know of her unrequited love, Joe knew. During one of the parties prior to the wedding, he led Lulu to the dance floor, then, barely into the dance, moved them out on to the terrace. He lit a cigarette and passed it to her, his eyes, full of sadness, never leaving hers.

Several times during the last year, Joe had called on Lulu to intercede on his behalf with Fanny, the butterfly who simply couldn't decide which of the many beaux she loved the most. Sometimes Lulu wasn't sure whether her heart hurt more for Joe or for herself. Now she stood beside him, he the star of her wildest imaginings, that *deus ex machina* she called upon when orgasm teased, and Joe would be there, his hands parting her thighs, and then his warm breath, his tongue, and she would explode.

"Think I'll be a good husband?" he asked.

"I thought you wanted to build that sailboat, cruise the Pacific, see the world."

Joe, the unflappable, looked suddenly close to tears. "I remember. You and Marcello and I were going to do that. Things don't always turn out as planned. I don't see Fanny carrying her clothes in a duffel. But you would, wouldn't you?"

Lulu was abruptly angry at him. She almost said, "Now you ask," but bit her tongue, looking more closely at the boy of her dreams. What the hell, she thought, I'll never get this chance again. "All my life I've dreamed about you. Don't ruin it for me, not at Fanny's wedding."

"Lousy timing. Funny about life, I loved being on my own and then you girls arrived. Zap, it all changed. It's great but it interrupted something I'll never get back."

"My best years, too, just before you guys turned up."

"Now I'm going to be a father."

"That boat in Tahiti…?"

"It'll have to wait…. Come on, Lulubelle… isn't that what March calls you? Come on, my Lulubelle, one last dance for old time's sake."

* * *

Two weeks before Lulu left for the West Coast, Harry telephoned, his voice full of eagerness to see her. "Your niece Delilah marks the calendar every day. 'Twelve more days 'til Aunt Lulu is here!' Only five years old and plays the piano better than I did at her age!"

"All my friends getting married, and I can't wait to be on my own."

"Wish I'd waited…oh, I love my daughter and all that…but you, Lulu, you've always been a girl who…well, it was written all over you. 'What does it all mean?' Now, you're gonna find out!"

They both laughed, Lulu a bit more sardonically. "Tell me about seeing Grandy…"

"Saw her last week. Listen to this! Out of the blue she starts talking about our father, said she knew we wanted to know more. Then she tells me how they ran into each other in London during the Blitz. There was an air raid, they were in a bar. He refused to go down to the shelter and dared her to stay with him. I couldn't tell how much she liked him. She did say he was wild and had a bad temper. 'But he was brave,' she gave him that, then added, 'You look like him, Harry,' said it in such a way I didn't know how to take it."

"She must have been amazing back then, both of them."

"Yeah…." Brother and sister were silent for a moment.

"I can't wait to see you…"

"Counting the days, little sister! Oh, by the way, don't expect Stella to be here. I didn't want to mention it in letters. She's not been here for over a year."

CHAPTER TWENTY-ONE

Harry was waiting when she got off the plane in Los Angeles. In the time it took to run across the tarmac and into his arms, she saw the change, not simply that he'd grown taller and his shoulders broader, but there was a solemnity about him. Harry was a grown-up man, handsome, serious-looking.

"Just look at you, Lu, my lovely little sister," and he held her at arm's length, searching her face. "Come on, let's get the bags and head for home. We'll cruise the movie star houses in Beverly Hills first, give us time to talk before little Delilah gets your ear. She's grown up on the lore of Lulu!"

They drove and talked until the old familiarity had returned, their shared childhood in a house of unanswered questions, each aware of what the other was thinking, spiritual in its way. Every once in a while Harry would reach over to touch her shoulder, squeeze her hand.

"This is where the movie stars live?" she asked as they drove down the immaculate, deserted streets of Beverly Hills, and then up higher into Bel Aire. "But we haven't seen a pedestrian. Where is everyone?"

"Nobody walks in L.A. It's against the law. Now we go home. Delilah must be wondering where we are."

Before they arrived at the house, he told her what Stella was up to in Alabama. "Chaperoned some black children from around here to be 'part of history,' as she put it. They did make the news, over a thousand of them singing the National Anthem outside the old confederate Capital."

"Good for Stella."

"It's heating up, *long overdue*. We'll talk about my busted marriage later. Now you meet your niece."

* * *

Little Venice was as exotic as its name, a maze of teeter-tottering houses, some of them more like shacks, Lulu was thinking, but wonderful, each painted a different color and set on stilts over the shallow water. "It's so, well, so different!" she said with delight, waiting for Harry to lead the way along the maze of footbridges.

But there was no missing the house, patrolled by a young girl in a pink dress. She ran to Harry's arms, never taking her eyes off Lulu. "Come to me, darlin', come to your aunt who's been dyin' to meet you," and the little girl broke from her father's arms and ran to Lulu's.

"I heard you play piano as well as your daddy," Lulu said, led by the child into the house where Delilah went directly to the piano.

"Go ahead, sweetheart," Harry said. "Delilah's composed a 'Welcome to Aunt Lulu' tribute."

"Only six years old and I bet you play like a dream!" Lulu went to sit beside her on the piano bench.

And so the evening went until Delilah reluctantly left Harry and Lulu for bed. Long into the night, brother and sister drank and talked about Penelope, Charleston, and Marcello's departure. About 3:00 a.m., having made a sizeable dent in the bottle of brandy, Lulu asked, "What really happened between you and Penelope in your bedroom?"

Perhaps because he was way ahead of her on the booze, Harry launched into the "nightmare, and it really was just that. Not much happened early on, though it was disconcerting, to put it mildly, having your mother tucked in behind you. But when I got older, her breasts pressed against my back, well they'd arouse me. I'd get a hard-on and I think she knew it. Then she heard through the grapevine that I had the hots for this beautiful black girl." Harry groaned, stabbing out his cigarette until it was pulp. "Anyway, one night she sort of crawled over me so that we were face to face. I was half-asleep and almost had my very erect penis inside her, until I heard her groaning my name. I'd been lost in fantasy that she *was* Stella—but her voice snapped me out of it. 'No, no!' I yelled, which I'd never done before, didn't dare. I made her leave. Right after that, Stella and I ran away."

Lulu was high on booze, exhausted, and shocked though she wasn't sure whether her outrage was for Harry or herself. All of her life she'd been jealous of him having their mother's undivided attention. She wanted to be furious at Penelope, but the words didn't come out that way.

"You had sex with our mother!" she said, an accusatory sound.

"You make it sound like I was the aggressor! Put my dick inside my mother? Dear God, Lulu, there's enough craziness in the family without…. Do you think I enjoyed those years, her coming to my bed? I *had* to run away, run as fast as I could!"

Brother and sister sat in silence, then Harry heaved a sigh, more like a groan, got up and took the bottle of booze to bed with him muttering, "…fucking women!"

Lulu sat alone, smarting that he'd turned on her, but even more focused on the rage roiling around inside her, rage that saw Harry's history with their mother in his bed as just another preferential decision that left her out, just like they'd left her behind when they went to see her father in the Dark City…. "No, no, don't dwell on it!" she ordered her thoughts. "Think of college, new beginnings."

The next morning, she couldn't piece it together, the booze and the time change confusing memory. When Harry and Delilah's voices woke her, Harry, thank God, sounded happy with his little girl.

Relieved that her world was intact, the next thoughts were, "She was on the other side of the world." This feeling of travel, new places, made her feel new herself, as in new identity, change, possibilities…yes, yes, she liked travel, and the word conjured up Grandy. Where would she be? Abruptly the door had just closed on Delilah's departure for day camp. Harry was trying to be quiet in the kitchen. She remembered their harsh last words the night before. Got to make this right with Harry. Can't fight, can't lose him, can't let him see my anger. "I love Harry!" she told herself. And in spite of last night—no, because she was schooled in putting a smiling face on a troubled soul—Lulu yawned loudly, got up, and joined her brother in the kitchen where she steered the conversation into safe waters. Over her second cup of coffee they were into talk of their blues opera and The Mansion.

"You wouldn't recognize certain parts of Charleston it's so spruced up," she said, relieved to hear the equanimity of her voice. "The town needs tourism money, but I hate seeing the dust removed. Tricky, isn't it, modernizing a place lost in time, but not killing its heart?"

"And The Mansion?"

'The families tell me that realtors have located the original people who owned the place before the Civil War. The families are worried they're going to lose the house. I did some research, learned there are 'squatters' rights.' You have to have lived in the house forty years to claim it's yours, and have a letter from the owners saying 'you can live here.' When the house was shelled at the end of the Civil War and the original family fled, that letter was given to one of the slaves who stayed. Supposedly a surviving relative who still lives on the top floor has the letter. But Harry, our musical is fiction, so we can have the black families fighting eviction...."

Harry got up and went to the piano. "Let me play you some rumble theme I've written for the black activists. And here's the music we hear from the white family next door, more or less our house. I sent copies of all this to Marcello. I like your idea of his working with us."

While Harry played, Lulu took him in, crouched over the keys in the little house with its worn furniture and walls covered with children's drawings, a poster announcing a voter registration rally in Alabama. If Penelope hadn't crawled into his bed, Lulu wondered, would he have ended up here? Instead, might he too be going to college? Compassion for her brother was bringing tears to her eyes when Harry hollered over the chords he was playing.

"Hey, kiddo, I haven't really written this yet, just improvising, getting the feel of it...."

Lulu went and stood behind him, her hands on his shoulders, and he turned and smiled up at her. "Can't think of anything I'd rather do, Lu, than write this musical with you and March." He reached up, took her hand and kissed it, the other hand never leaving the keyboard. "And here's the ballad, a paean of love of place, of heritage which is counterpart to the sexual love between the beautiful white girl and the black boy gone north to fight in Freedom Summer."

"Harry, Harry," Lulu was near tears of delight. "When we first started talking about this, I thought you were just going along to please me...."

"Maybe in the beginning, but no more. It stays with me, y'know, in the back of my head even when I'm working on something else."

"The families in the mansion, they really do want to relocate them into these pre-fab boxes. It's a virus creeping all over Charleston, everything being prettified. I know the town needs money, but..."

"Our story's not alone. If I hadn't been thinking about it, maybe I'd not have noticed what they're tearing down here in L.A. all in the name of 'Progress.'"

"Hey, that's a good work title, 'Progress' or maybe 'Lost Charleston...' how about a love song for the black boy and his white sweetheart?"

"A crescendo of their love ballad when he gets killed in Korea." Harry's heavy chords dive into a discordant heartbreak.

"...and the big, ominous wrecking ball?"

"Yes, yes, it swings across the stage with its own music, the enormous black ball on its chain," and he plays the chords, huge and menacing.

"And the old island spirituals?"

"Plus a little Gershwin, a little Joplin?"

"The villain is greed, the developers in bed with the politicians! And to show we're not unreasonable, we have a theme of '*good* progress,' as in the anthem for Civil Rights. And, Harry, lots of love songs!"

"Amen, Lulu, amen."

"You're amazing! How do you make up music as you go along?"

"Out here, auditioning, you only get a few minutes, so you give 'em what they want, you hope. We'll get more of this in later," Harry promised. "Cross your fingers for me. I've a big audition in half an hour."

After he left, Lulu dialed Grandy's number on the East Coast. But her houseman said Grandy was out of town. When Lulu identified herself, he announced, "Why, Miss Lulu, she's in Los Angeles, too!" and he gave her the number of the Bel Aire Hotel.

"God is smiling down upon us!" Grandy exclaimed when Lulu called. "Come to lunch with me."

Lulu and Grandy spent most of the day at The Bel Aire Hotel, "an oasis in heaven," as Lulu proclaimed it. They drank Negronis out by the enormous pool surrounded by exotic palms and Birds of Paradise, and had lunch under the umbrellas served by men in white coats. Grandy kept to the shade, her hand occasionally reaching over to stroke Lulu's wet hair. Lulu floated in the pool, studying her grandmother's beauty for the first time. In her own habitat, relaxed, she held herself like a queen. "Why, Grandy, you have a ring on your toe!" Lulu exclaimed.

"Oh, that, yes, your and my birthstone, opal. Here, you take it." She removed the toe ring and handed it to Lulu. "Don't say 'oh, I can't' to me. And now that we've exhausted family gossip, tell me what subjects you're taking at college." This topic eventually segued to Penelope and "that dreadful Admiral," Grandy's words.

"I'm loathe to protest too much," Grandy sighed, "as it simply fans the flames of that romance. I've put some men on his case, a little detective work. Penelope wouldn't recognize a four-flusher if he pawned her jewelry. Our Admiral spent a lot of time in Cuba recently, and I don't think he was sightseeing. Can't imagine he's friendly with Castro, but you never know."

"Just before I left Charleston," Lulu said, "I saw him down at the waterfront with the captain of a freighter that had just docked. They were unloading some big wooden boxes. Mother let him store them in our basement."

"You mean, his, along with my boxes? The nerve of that bastard. He just wants an excuse to go down there… Sorry, Lulu."

"Don't apologize to me, Grandy. I feel the same way about him."

Grandy sighed. "Sometimes I think the only reason Penelope chose him is my dislike of the bastard."

"You're so generous to me, Grandy. I'm grateful but…this is hard to say and I know March wouldn't want…."

"Spit it out, Lulu."

"He works so hard on his music…the show he's writing…and I know he needs money and he'd never ask…."

Grandy sat back in her chair, toyed with the fork in front of her. "You're right. Marcello's been generous to you and I'm grateful. Stop worrying, I'll send him a check. He's lucky you…."

"No! You don't understand…I owe my life to Marcello. I love him more…."

Grandy changed the subject. "I'm off to Washington in a few days. I detest Joe Kennedy, but I backed Jack. Something original about him, the kind of man who'll grow quickly into his role, hopefully a great President."

"And Jackie?"

"Glad you brought her up. Mention Jackie and I think clothes. Did Penelope outfit you properly for college?"

Lulu's mouth opened and closed. "I don't need new clothes, Grandy."

"I thought as much. I'm not having you at a fine women's college looking like a latchkey child. Clothes aren't everything, but attractive wrappings help. Early beauty is a curse. You stop honing skills, get used to adulation for just standing there. Late bloomers like you and me, well, beauty is a gift."

"Grandy, you've already given me…"

"Tomorrow we go to Neiman's. I'll call my woman to put some things together. Don't look worried, this is going to be fun. I promise not to say a word of rebuke to Penelope."

When Grandy and Lulu arrived at Neiman Marcus the next day, the saleswoman rolled out several racks of dresses, skirts, sweaters, shoes, even underwear. "Not a word!" Grandy warned, "just throw yourself into it as though it were a movie."

Dressed in one beautiful outfit after another, Lulu stared judgmentally at her reflection for the first time. She had ceded the mirror to Penelope and her own beautiful friends, her self-image having to do with action, words, anything but beauty, a child's pyric victory. In her mind's eye, there was nothing she could do to make her mother see her. So painful was invisibility, she had turned it around; it was *she* who neither saw nor needed Penelope. But today's mirror was kind, and Lulu considered extending her list of what mattered.

The fashion show finished, Grandy ordered two large pieces of luggage. "I'll have them pack your clothes and send them to Radcliffe so they arrive when you do. The luggage is Louis Vuitton and will last a lifetime. Weighs a ton but you're a girl who won't be long without a strong man at her side."

They had lunch at The Brown Derby where Grandy waved to Peter Lawford who rose and blew her a kiss. Later, Humphrey Bogart stopped at their table to say hello.

"You know movie stars?" Lulu asked with awe.

I've been backing films since my third husband in the late Forties," Grandy said.

Out of the blue, emboldened by her second Margarita, Lulu asked, "Did you know my father well, Grandy?"

But her grandmother stiffened and in a voice never before used with Lulu said, "This is for your mother to discuss with you."

The tone, more than the message, was a harsh reprimand. Last night with Harry had left her vulnerable. Now another door was slammed in her face by someone she loves. What could be so awful that everyone but her knew the secret?

After lunch they drove to a place called Santa Monica where Grandy had a meeting, along the way passing several demolition sites. Still deeply upset, Lulu had not said a word since leaving the restaurant. "They're destroying everything that was beautiful," Grandy sighed, staring out the window. "Not just here but in the city of L.A. as well. What's got into people?"

"They're tarting up everything in Charleston, too."

"It's not just buildings we're losing, it's our way of life, manners, tradition. Dearest Lulu, I'm sorry I barked at you earlier. I must get out here. Charles will take you back."

Lulu made an effort, more self-preservation than gratitude. "Grandy, won't you come with us tonight? Harry's taking me to the club where he's playing. It would be wonderful if the three of us could be together."

"You're absolutely right. What's the name of the club?"

"Shelley's Mann Hole. I'll phone you directions."

"Oh, Shelley and I are old friends. I hope Jerry Mulligan's playing. I'll be there around ten. Don't look surprised, the real night life doesn't start until then."

Driving back to Harry's, Lulu felt her first ambivalence towards her grandmother. Why does even Grandy leave me out of my father's story? How old must I be before they tell me? Then her thoughts drifted to The Bad Admiral, Sly's remarks that he had spent time in Cuba, and Lulu remembered a few years ago seeing Grandy and the Admiral arguing at the waterfront in Charleston. Was he storing guns in our basement? And there were the foreigners Sly said the Admiral had brought to the place where Josie worked, "shady types," Sly had called them. Shady, indeed. "We're closing in on you, you rat," Lulu thought.

CHAPTER TWENTY-TWO

Lulu sat on Delilah's bed and asked if she were too old for a bedtime story. "Not if you tell it," said the girl.

"Here's my favorite story," Lulu began. "One day your daddy and Marcello and I are going to make this story into a musical for Broadway. It's about a little girl your age who lives in a big pink house down south. One night when everyone is asleep, the little girl crawls out of her bedroom window and drops onto a high wall. She hears singing and laughter close by, and crawls along the wall until she comes to an enormous tree where she sits so that she can see the source of all the fun. And there they are, several families with many children who live in an old mansion next door. They are very, very poor, and one day some bad people threaten to throw them out unless they can find enough money to buy it. So the little girl from the pink house decides to write a musical show with her brother and charge people admission to see the singing and dancing. So the brother and sister write a story and music to go with it and they put it on a stage and people come. They raise enough money to buy the house so the families can live there...."

"And they lived happily ever after?"

"When you come to Charleston, you'll see how happy they are. We'll visit them."

When Lulu returned to the living room, Harry was lighting a joint which he passed to her. "Wow, great dope," she tried for sophistication.

"Hits you right away." They began to talk about music, a theme they stayed with in the car on the way to Shelly's Man Hole.

"I'm glad you asked Grandy to come along tonight," Harry said. "She's had people come to hear me play. What a woman!"

The mood was so right and her closeness to Harry as an equal seemingly so sure, Lulu blurted out, "Tell me a little more about our father."

"Oh, shit, Lulu, not now! Last night you bring up that business about my mother in my bed and now *him*. Ask Grandy."

"She won't talk about him either. Anyway, Grandy didn't know him that well...."

"Sure she did. They were good friends. I told you about when I was little and he used to take me everywhere? Sometimes he took me to see Grandy. I loved being with them because they laughed a lot. He and mother, that could be tense. But with Grandy, well, even a little kid likes to see the true man, his dad..."

"What did they talk about?"

"Horses, oh, and paintings, art. Yeah, they talked a lot about Grandy collecting art. It was '42, the war had just begun, Grandy had signed up for some branch of the Special Services, and our dad was already in uniform, one of the first to go."

Lulu was sorry they'd arrived at Shelly's. This was a story she'd have liked to go on forever, a happy image of two people she loved.

Shelly's was in downtown L.A., and the place was packed, the music amplified by the grass they'd smoked. Harry pointed out the musicians, Jerry Mulligan on clarinet, trumpet player Art Farmer, base player Bill Crow, and Shelley Mann himself on drums. It was so smoky inside that Lulu's eyes watered, but the music more than made up for it.

"Tell them that Grandy's coming," Lulu told Harry. Then he joined the group, and the music soared. Lulu lit up with pleasure, not having heard him play since The Hot Spot. Somewhere during the evening, Shelley put his Chinese cymbal on his head and was playing the drums as if the sticks were chopsticks. But that was the least of the hilarity. About midnight, Harry took Lulu out back where some grass was being passed around. A few tokes later, they went back inside just as Grandy walked in.

"There's my grandmother!" said Lulu excitedly to the base player Bill Crow.

"You're related to Grandy, you lucky girl?" Lulu had to wait her turn to embrace her grandmother who was escorted by two men.

More time passed as the crowd pulled together, a passionate congregation not unlike Church in Charleston, Lulu was thinking. Her arm was around Grandy, the center of attention at their table. The musicians clearly loved her and Lulu basked in the way they looked at her grandmother.

Harry had been playing brilliantly, ripping through a wild version of "I Get Along Without You Very Well," then "There Will Never Be Another You." Now when he stood, however, he stumbled on his way to the men's room.

"That's some grass they're smoking in there," Lulu said to a musician sitting beside her.

"Honey, that ain't smoke." The man made a gesture of a needle being jabbed into his arm.

Lulu froze. Only in movies had she seen this, and they'd all ended badly.

When Harry returned, Grandy sat beside him on the piano bench. The next time Harry rose to make his way to the men's room, he grabbed Grandy's hand and took her with him, leaving Lulu alone as the rest of the room applauded.

Smoking grass was one thing, but from what Lulu had seen in the movies, heroin wasn't something you could take or leave. Heroin was an addiction. People died. Lulu's world was a balloon held up by Grandy and Harry and, on a good day, maybe herself. But now an injection of another sort flooded her system: "Grandy and Harry had formed a union and left me out!" The rage inside boiled and revenge took precedence. How dare they leave her out! Fury looked for a weapon with which to punish them, but the only tool was to walk out and she stood, pushed towards the front door, high as a kite on self-righteousness.

She hadn't seen Grandy exit the men's room the moment after she'd entered, didn't see her grandmother take a quick bow and then allow herself to be stopped by laughing friends on her way back to the table.

By that time, Lulu had found a taxi and was on her way back to Harry's, her mind packed with fury, grief, the old left-out feeling and, yes, revenge. She was half-sorry she'd left Shelly's, but the other half scoffed at her questioning: "Let them worry," her hurt self said. "How could they do that to me in front of all those people? Leave me out, go away together, close the door in my face? They'll be sorry!"

Before Harry stumbled into the house she was ashamed she'd left the party. "Where does it come from?," she asked herself, all my killer fury when someone slights me? I'm like a bomb waiting to go off and it's always been there. Was I born angry, like the girl in "The Bad Seed?" "Dear Lord, please don't let me get my father's disease." When Harry opened the door an hour later, he made no effort to be quiet.

"You're not asleep, you little brat. You're so fucking self-centered, walking out on Grandy! You've no idea how you hurt the person who loves you more than…"

"Go to bed, you addict," Lulu snarled. "You're doing heavy drugs and…"

"Not your damn business. Cut the shit, Lulu. You've always been jealous. You set it up for me and Grandy to get together so she can help me, then you hate it when you see how well it's worked. Grandy'll forgive you—already has—was in tears…."

Harry had never spoken to her in this voice, and Lulu's resentment blazed. "I don't recognize you."

"You and Stella! God help me."

That did it. What with the left over pain from Shelly's, her remorse at punishing them by running out like a little girl, along with self-defense at doing so, Lulu bit into the resentment of Harry felt all her life, and took a big mouthful. Oh, he'd made it joyful, too, but alongside was this other venomous feeling. God, she hated him!

"You spoiled little boy!" she yelled. "Okay, so you didn't actually screw your mommy, but you let her lie against you night after night! You enjoyed it!"

Harry mumbled, "Go to hell," and stumbled into his room, slamming the door.

Lulu lay in the dark nursing her fury, a lifetime of envying the very person for whose love she had built the dam to keep it at bay. Now it roiled like thunder, jealousy joined by the reminder of what she'd also done to Grandy…or was it what Grandy had done to her? Back and forth the emotions argued, but what they kept coming back to was her need of Grandy—and Harry, too.

In the dark of the unfamiliar room far from home, Lulu hugged herself, bile and rage running concurrently. Then from another estuary came guilt and remorse that neither Grandy nor Harry would ever love her again.

It was too much to sleep with. She lay there, trying to understand why she couldn't control her need to get even when…when what? When someone leaves me…. But other people get rejected and they don't go crazy, she reasoned. Don't use the crazy word! she ordered herself. Half a dozen times she thought of getting in a cab and going to Grandy. By the time she heard Delilah and Harry get up, tiptoe around so as not to wake her, the rage had been captured down into that dark, dank place where it had always lived. Her jaw had locked from gnashing her teeth in the night.

She heard Harry and Delilah leave, the car start and the sound of the tires diminish. He would be back in an hour. Time to telephone Grandy, apologize. But when Lulu telephoned, a servant said Grandy had left early on a trip and wouldn't be back for several weeks.

Lulu waited tensely until Harry returned. "I'm sorry, Harry," she said. "I'm so sorry about what happened last night. If you stop loving me…."

"I could no more stop loving you than stop loving music." He sat her down opposite him on the sofa. "Don't ever be jealous of me and Grandy."

"Did she see my stupid jealousy?"

"God, no. She was higher than either of us, mostly on joy just being with us. I promise you, Lulu, no one will ever take your place in her heart or mine."

"I hope I grow out of this."

And she managed a smile as they sang the refrain of "My Funny Valentine" together.

But chagrin at what she'd done stayed even after Harry had put her on the airplane to Boston. How could she feel such rage at the people she loved most? She remembered asking him about their father. Boy, her timing's really something, she thought. Then self-rebuke turned to a picture of Harry shooting heroin into his arm, an horrific image. No more dark thoughts, she ordered herself. Think of college, think of falling in love with a boy who loves you back.

CHAPTER TWENTY-THREE

Scholastically, socially, emotionally Lulu was unprepared for Radcliffe. It was a stunning setback. Here was a population of women who'd been training all their lives, primed, focused, hungry for it as soldiers. They, too, had been president of their class, captain of the team, best in everything. From her first day, survival was all Lulu could hope for. She became a loner and relished the invisibility.

But the homesickness was profound, and she was grateful for the work, all day, evenings and weekends of blinding concentration. When grades came, she was shocked. "I've never worked so hard," she told her advisor. "Try harder," the woman said.

As fall lengthened, so did her shadow on the sidewalk, long and dark, a menacing Ichabod of a shadow. The dark Lulu. She'd use that dark part of herself, it would be her "dark ink" to help her become the writer she knew she could be. "Lulu, in Charleston, you were so intent on being Miss Sweetness and Light. Ever consider why you had to be everybody's best friend, never alone? Well, consider it now."

The only exception to her studies was an evening job on weekends at a local bookstore. She refused to ask Grandy for more money. I won't be like mother, she vowed. I won't ever, ever stand with my hand out.

* * *

The call from Penelope came just one week before Lulu was to leave for Charleston for Thanksgiving. One of the girls in the dorm knocked on her door to tell her that her mother was on the hall phone. "Now don't be upset, dear" she started, "but I've decided to sell the house and marry the Admiral. We are going to Key West for our honeymoon and then on to the Admiral's new assignment. Of course we've known our plans for a few months but also knowing how it would upset you, we decided it would be better for all of us if we waited until you had settled in at school to tell you."

The betrayal was too much. She couldn't inhale, couldn't form words. What boiled up was an enormous wave of grief and rage. All the sadness of never being seen or feeling love from her mother now gathered up in a gagging bile that rose from deep inside her.

"How can you do this to me?", she growled, teeth clenched." You have always known what Charleston is to me, you never wanted me, never gave me comfort, but turned all that greedy neediness of yours onto Harry… scaring him, terrifying him".

"Oh, Lulu…" Penelope stammered, her words more full of self-pity than anger or any other emotion.

"Don't you understand, Mother? Don't you get it?… but no, you never even cared enough about me to be jealous now when I tell you that <u>the place</u>, Charleston is my family. Why didn't you tell me before I left that you were leaving? Why, why? I will never forgive you for playing this trick on me. Get Lulu out of town and dump this on her. Shame on you!" Lulu slammed down the phone.

Lulu sat in the tiny booth, staring at the phone, waiting for her breathing to stop pounding in her chest. She had never spoken to her mother in the tone of voice that still filled the tiny cramped space in which she sat. "Comfort", she said aloud, "I need someone to tell me I'm not crazy. I need someone…" and Marcello's name filled the space, as she quickly dialed his number. When his voice sounded in her head crowded with emotion, just her word , "March…" and then his voice naming her, already knowing she was in danger and needed him.

"Lulu, dearest girl, I'm here. Talk to me."

Lulu swallowed, inhaled deeply and spoke slowly, gathering her words.

"She betrayed me March. She waited until I was gone and then struck. She knew I wouldn't leave Charleston if I knew her plan. She wanted to tuck me away up north, here and then make her move… take away everything and everyone who really matter to me. I'm going back, March. I'll go to college in Charleston…"

"Lulu, my darling girl, listen to me. I can feel what you feel. I take in your words deep inside. Believe me when I say they are mine and that I am feeling just what you feel. That's how you must think of it right now. I feel every ounce of your outrage and fear of losing the only mother you've ever known. And that place is your mother. It saved you. It grew you and loved you back."

"Oh, I knew you'd understand, Marcello… Thank you, thank you.…"

"Now listen to me , my darling. Every mother that raises a child, every bird, every animal, raises its young to leave the nest. That place, not Penelope, has done its job. Don't you see? If you didn't repay Charleston by taking courage in hand and proving the brilliance of that intelligence, that grand mind of yours that Charleston fostered… why sweetheart, forget about Penelope! Think of the place and what you owe it…"

There was a long silence and then a very little girl voice. "I am going home and that is that." Lulu hung up the phone, and soaked in tears went back to her room.

* * *

The elegant Vuitton luggage that only weeks ago was carefully unpacked, the garments full of expectations as she hung each piece like a promise, a symbol of the years ahead, now she grabbed the lot of them, stuffing them pell mell into the open suitcases.

Her lips were moving as she intentionally threw the clothes atop one another. "Damn the clothes, damn the college, damn them all," she hissed aloud through clenched teeth. "Grandy is no heroine," she said aloud, in full voice. "I made her into a heroine I needed and now she's proven her real self. What a silly girl I was…and as for Harry, boy, I sure can pick 'em…me and my heros.… As God is my witness…"

She stopped, stood erect and began to laugh out loud; so loud, so hard a laugh that the sad tears turned to celebration.

"Oh my God, listen to me!" she said. "Oh, Lulu, you're quoting Scarlett O'Hara in "Gone With the Wind!." And she lay on the floor with the unpacked clothes clasped to her breast, "Oh, Scarlett, honey, just like you I've got my test in front of me. Oh great goddess of lost girls who would-be-heroines, you are giving me a giant challenge. Very well, if this is my supreme test, I accept. So I absolutely cannot go back to Charleston a failure. OK, I've got this far. I'm away from home. So, it hasn't turned out the way I expected. Well, that too is part of the test. One thing I do know, I can't be like my mother, a lovely woman, but a woman with her hand out depending on the kindness of strangers. So, Damn it! I'll stay in this place, get the best education if it kills me. Then, I'll go back to Charleston, not to marry a rich man, but to invent myself, to buy my own pink house, with my own money. And God help us all!"